SONG OF THE TEMPLAR

Nigel Clayton

First Published in Australia by Zuytdorp Press in 2020

The National Library of Australia Cataloguing-in-Publication data:
Clayton, Nigel. Song of the Templar, 1st ed.
ISBN 9780648767299

FIC009100 FICTION / Fantasy / Action & Adventure
POE014000 POETRY / Epic
POE022000 POETRY / Medieval

Epic Poems by this Author:

Kibeho: An Epic Poem
Afghan - Song of the Desert
Orcinus Orca - Song of the Ocean
Hollandia Nova, 1712 - Song of the Coast
Song of the Templar

Novels:

Dreamtime: An Aboriginal Odyssey
Templar, Assassination, Trial & Torture

NOTE:

This epic poem is drawn directly from the words of Templar, Assassination, Trial & Torture: written in verse.

About the Author:

Nigel joined the Australian Army in 1980 at age 17yrs and 2 months, and after completing training at Kapooka was whisked away to the School of Infantry, Singleton, New South Wales, Australia.

He served in the Infantry until injury forced a medical discharge upon him in 1996, after having served in Southeast Asia, 1982; PNG (with the AATPT - Australian Army Training Project Team), in 1990: during the Bougainville Crisis; and in Rwanda, 1995: known world-wide for the Kibeho Massacre which occurred on April 22 nd of that year.

He was married in 1999 and has two children.

Chapter One

25th October, 1314, a period in history filled with gore,
And here we see the gaoler pushing knight heavily to floor,
He locks the cell door most securely behind,
A sinister smile upon his face so easy to find.

This gaoler, a fool, always content,
Happy to issue pain with threats so easily lent,
Eager to cause misery to fall upon others,
Young children and old, fathers and mothers.

The dungeon was one of the darkest in France,
Or supposedly so, its character seen at a glance,
But shards of light penetrated adequately enough,
For us all to grasp understanding, of a man so tough.

Bernard de Beauvais, Knights Templar, man so bold,
Was thankful for the few mercies, mercies here told,
The first, being provided him by nature's sweetest gift,
To be provided a fresh breeze, from somewhere, a rift.

And upon the breeze came a most heavenly fragrance,
One he'd smelt before, but not recall, before this durance,
It smelt quite heavenly, as though a reward for past endeavour,
Or was he simply disorientated, dreaming: no, no, no; never.

He lifted his head and drew the fragrance in deeply,
Towards his lungs… it was, sure enough, quite simply,
Such a beautiful thing to feel free about,
To give to the world a lofty shout.

But who would hear him, no one for sure,
None came near such a place, there existed no lure,
No lure made by man's sacred hand,
Nowhere to be seen upon this land.

This fragrance, seemingly bold, to visit him now,
When he needed it most, a great weight lifted from brow,
The tissue of his face falling with ease,
Relaxed enough, enough to tease.

For he knew, he was powerless to do anything of his situation,
One so pathetically cruel, so heinous, at turmoil his frustration,
To be flung so deliberately and with such careless action,
By the hands of his gaoler: pain his pleasure, his passion.

Yes, by his greasy hands, into this cell, of the gaoler,
Preference there was to be set in chains at galley by sailor,
Such dirty hands had likely never seen a hard day's work,
Torturing victims, methods orchestrated, from shadows he lurk.

Bernard's second mercy came from his gaoler's hand,
Before into this cell so confined, wearing unwarranted brand,
For Bernard had a crust of bread stuffed beneath his shirt,
One that he hungered for, a hunger so strong that it hurt.

His gaolers had failed to find this sweet, tiny morsel,
During the interval of their searching, being abysmal,
For they were more concerned over the weapon,
The one he carried by his side, of the best iron.

And what of the short knife strapped to his lower leg,
Ah! This one Bernard made sure they found, no need to beg,
Simply cause a small, unnecessary action,
Enough to create that sufficient distraction.

So easy, you see, to draw away the eye,
So easy for Bernard to act, the truth to deny,
Drawing the sheet over their eyes, this deceit,
And for no trouble at all held some bread as a receipt.

Bernard pushed his hand into the hiding place of his clothing,
His main vestment stolen, gaolers also drawing his loathing,
For the cross on his vestment was sewn upon his heart,
There to the finish, from the very start.

After a short breath he pulled the bread from its hiding,
Something to take comfort in, in which to be abiding,
Though such abiding was nought compared to his trust,
In his conviction to Order, in which his life he did thrust.

He looked upon it with great satisfaction: he did stare,
Just, barely, able to make out the outline of his ware,
Seeing not clearly its poor condition, so pressed as it was,
Though strong was his need, coursing through body a buzz.

It was sour to look at, now more hard biscuit than anything,
Not appealing to the eye, its true semblance would sting,
It was then that another prisoner, from the adjoining cell,
Suddenly broke his silence, breaking that silent spell.

“Ahem; I see you have something there,”
Came the crackled sound of an old man amidst his stare,
A voice telling the tale of many hours of torture,
His nose twitching at a smell foretelling of future.

Yes, such a smell he’d not caught for some time,
One enough to lift his spirits from the brime,
And with his sight having adapted to the poor light,
He could see more clearly within the dungeon of little delight.

There the essence of madness was strung upon every word,
A voice, whether hoarse or otherwise, so easily heard,
This poor man, owner of an array of sounds whilst speaking,
His vocal cords having clearly taken a beating.

He’d been sleeping and was now awake,
From his unsteady slumber he did now shake,
Only slightly awakened by the shutting of cell door,
The gaoler having retreated from the misery and more.

The old man staggered to his feet,
From his bench, a bed with no sheet,
He had trouble gaining secure footing,
For he was weak, from within he was hurting.

He was stooping as any old man may stoop,
But his more pitiful and wretched, but still he swoop,
Quite quick with wit,
Like a snake, ready to spit.

Bernard looked up and over to the shifting silhouette,
To the crouched and hungry man in the shadows, no threat,
Here the shadows moved, hard to see and very poor,
Drifting here and there, of what to see, Bernard was unsure.

And then the skeleton form of injustice came into full fruition,
The blur came upon a portion of clarity: the lack of nutrition,
Here the barest of light fell his way from a crack from door,
A small gift from within a large crack, and with aid he saw.

Bernard felt sorry for the old man at that moment in time,
But needed to be concerned for himself: was this a crime?
If he didn't attend to his needs first then he would surely die,
Within the walls of this cell, a truth he could not deny.

Bernard was quick with mind, quick with wit,
With him many choices, upon his mind they sit,
Much to deliberate upon in short span,
Easy answer, easy reply, rely on life's plan.

An undernourished body didn't feed the bowls of knowledge,
There was no lack of poor service in neglect so pledge,
He'd learnt this during his many years of servitude,
To his Order and religion, neither of which could he elude.

"You look like you haven't eaten for some time, old man,"
Said Bernard to the wretched sight: help where you can,
Give to the poor where they need it the most,
Give freely of honour and try never to boast.

"My name is Aimery, I've been here for two long years,
Less food has passed my lips, during this time, or so it appears,
Two months on the streets of Paris would feed me as well,
Would be more worthy than any time spent here in hell."

Can a man grow accustomed to poor treatment,
From within this darkest of holes so easily sent,
Bernard felt the staleness of the loaf in his hand,
So hard, lack of essence, what was once so grand.

If he kept it all for himself... could he live with that decision?
A reminder again: do not act poorly, to do so is treason,
He'd served crusaders of all walks, no individual cast in frame,
Forever and a day it would seem; to pity them all the same.

"Do the years within this… sacred palace, with bench for bed,
Qualify you for a portion of my most… humble of bread?"
Bernard spoke these words as his eyes peered to the right,
His peripheral gifting more clarity to the dreadful sight.

"A single day in this place, palace or not,
Deserves recognition, please do not let me rot,
Let alone a week, a month, or a year,
My hunger does taunt me with its ugly sneer. "

Aimery added further clarity to his spoken word,
He licked his lips, ready for action, as though to gird,
"I haven't had good bread in so long,
I forget what it tastes like, but my hope is strong."

Bernard wished to know more,
To understand this man, to be sure,
"I wish to ask of your life's segment,
What's the date of your imprisonment?"

"Ah; I can't recall... not by first inwards glance,
But before King Edward's marriage to Isabella of France,
The daughter of that bastard of a man, King Philip."
And here was the clarification, loss of sanity, loss of grip.

Bernard looked into the depths of insanity,
The looming forgetfulness of the old man: what a pity,
The obvious dilemma he was now in,
Of the injustices suffered, it was all, pure sin.

Bernard stepped forward to grasp a better understanding,
To take a better look at this dying man, of his aging,
To become better learned of this poor creature's soul,
Aimery so painfully stooped before him, of life and its toll.

"Then you have been here for six long summers, to the year,
Not two as you suspect," announced Bernard without cheer,
And a spark came over Aimery, possibly fear,
The fruition of his being came into gear.

"Not two," Aimery suddenly found strength within,
And his arm was thrust through the bars amidst evil grin,
Through the space which separated the two adjoining cells,
Spittle flying from the jaws of his decaying mouth: he smells.

The stinking breath of his exhaled gasp,
The vibration of vocals to throat a rasp,
Falling upon the heavenly knight,
But he stepped back with no sign of fright.

Soiled now, as though a beautiful maiden of position,
As though soiled by mud, or rotten tomatoes of poor nutrition,
Each thrown the maiden's way in an attempt to deprave,
Aimery's actions and condition… to soon be in the grave.

"Give me some of that bread, you filthy vermin!"
Clear cut and simple, no sermin,
He was clearly, quite insane, this poorly kept cell his home,
Aimery was exhausted in body and mind, tired to the bone.

Bernard was a little shocked, this clearly different than fright,
Which was surprising when considering he was a knight,
The ordeals of life thrown him during service to his Order,
Decades of noble strength and courage he did shoulder.

Was all he had achieved, for this day,
Was this the culmination, of his stay,
Was his last days on earth to be so sour,
Was he to be inturned here or tortured in tower.

Bernard stood silently and arrived upon a mindful decision,
For such arrived fast to a man of true wit and determination,
He stepped casually towards the man's outreached arm,
Gone all hint of caution, gone all alarm.

For Aimery's need was obviously more than his own,
Bernard offered the bread, handing it gently, not thrown,
But fast he was to withdraw it, retrieved without fanfare,
Aimery's rasped claw of a hand snatching amidst evil stare.

Aimery sounded like a hungry beast more than anything,
Penetrating noises of hunger rising, ready to sting,
The food shoved unceremoniously into aged mouth and jaw,
It lasted but mere seconds before Aimery collapsed on floor.

He stretched out his arms with a smile,
He was momentarily contented within, no denial,
His grin pasted wide across his face,
Looking like Jesus laid flat and filled with grace.

Said Bernard: "I'm glad you can enjoy it,"
As he wiped from his face a little grime, a little spit,
The old man looked up from there upon the floor of his cell,
"Enjoy it! It was like heaven to me; what more can I tell."

And Aimery continued in his good humour,
None too late, and neither, none the sooner,
“Who are you, to come here with bread hidden, this secret,
Dressed in clean clothing still fresh from the washing basket?”

And he spat out a tooth,
So loosened by the truth,
Of his vigorous rage upon the meal,
One so true and not surreal.

Bernard peered up and down, considered himself filthy,
Saw how the old man viewed him differently: so wealthy,
For the rags that Aimery wore were falling from his skin,
The skeleton that they clung to was so desperately thin.

“I’m a knight,” said Bernard, clear and straight to the point,
A voice so proud to announce, as a bishop would anoint,
“A knight; hmm; you don’t look much like a knight to me, ”
Aimery said, “and so easy it is for me to see.

“You’re too old to be a knight; too fat around the face,
You cannot be a fighting man, not a man of real grace,
Your hair is so grey; and that beard: no knight wears such,
No; you’re too old to be a knight; it’s not true; it’s too much.”

“Fat around the face, ah? Maybe it’s you who’s too thin,”
Bernard said, and thereafter believing he’d committed a sin,
No sooner had those words escaped him and Aimery was back,
Upon his feet, reaching through the bars, again on the attack.

He endeavoured again to claw at Bernard's flesh,
"You scum, bastard," spat Aimery, wishing to beat, to thresh,
"You filthy whore; come closer you shit; you homesexual,
You should be drawn and quartered for being so... sensual."

Bernard sat down upon the wooden bench so short,
Attached to the wall, to gather some thought,
Away from this little, angry man,
To consider something pleasant, a plan.

Bernard could see that he was insane,
This was too easy to see, too plain,
He would do well to stay clear and out of his reach,
For crazy men had strength and power, and little to teach.

"I am a Knights Templar, as true a knight as ever did live."
Aimery had settled down once more from attack, none to give,
He was quick to temper and quick to embrace calm, to console,
He lifted an ear to the sound of some jingling: the toll, the toll.

"Hmm, sounds like someone has taken a liking to you, my pet,
The gaoler is coming to see you; the one already met."
Bernard said: "Maybe he's come to see you; it's you he wants."
"No, my dear," insisted Aimery, "it's you: he loves savants."

Asked Bernard cheekily: "Do you always treat visitors kindly?
Have you always been so pleasant, always this friendly?"
Said Aimery: "You're the first in many months that I've seen,
Truly; of company I am not truly fond, nor am I keen.

"I've only been brought up here so they can torture me a little,
For I heard them once say I am simple, rather brittle and fickle,
But now it's your turn to dine with the hangman, this gaoler,
In his chamber of secrets, whose methods see no failure."

"And to think that I've only just arrived," bravely said Bernard,
"How kind of them, " and stood in readiness to meet the ward,
Said Aimery: "The man with chains is coming; you'll see,
He's going to dice you, with the Spanish Tickler; hehehehe. "

Aimery suddenly changed his tone and his eyes lit up,
"That bastard little shit will be here soon, on pain to sup,
Quick; hide, don't let him see you," and he went scurrying,
Running around in circles, fearing the foreboding.

The dungeon door burst open and there stood the gaoler,
With a candle held aloft his head, this beast, this empaler,
His head swaying a little to the left and then right,
Gaining a better look upon the interior, this bearer of light.

"Shut your noise, you little creep, or it's you I'll destroy,
I'll introduce you - you'll see - to my latest toy."
He was here to annoy,
He was here for joy.

Aimery stopped dead in his tracks, stood there, a statue,
What could he say or do: just don't argue,
With his eyes wide open he looked the gaoler in the face,
Dumbness pasted across him: "I'll be good," no shred of grace.

"You, the knight, get your arse over here," ordered the gaoler,
He unlocked the door to Bernard's cell: there was none viler,
A smirk fell upon Aimery's face, locking eyes with the knight,
Bernard stepped up to the cell door, towards the candlelight.

"Move it," said the gaoler as Bernard pushed past,
Out into the corridor where two men were ready for task,
They grabbed him from either side, these two oxen,
The dungeon door shut but the cell door left open.

Said Aimery, more to self, so mad and demented,
"Oh, so be it, to be taken away," so dimwitted,
Twisted in body, mind and soul, never to be free,
"Hehe; such a bastard is that gaoler; hmm; the knight will see."

Chapter Two

Bernard was forced along, manhandled, through passages cold,
No gentle warmth here, of none to be told,
Ushered in such rough manner in order to secure their trophy,
To maintain their vigorous dominion: their only philosophe.

The deadly gloom of his predicament was hence revealed,
More clarity forming in his mind as each step was peeled,
His future drawing nearer although slightly unclear,
It was forming well and drew very, very near.

He was innocent all any charge,
Either small or even large,
But he was a Templar, and that was acknowledgement alone,
That the hangman's gallows was here, to become his throne.

His mind was alight with further episodes of torture,
Torture he had endured over the years, to loath, not nurture,
Nothing more than memories which he didn't wish to see again,
Pain issued by the hand of Muslims in forsaken lands a stain.

Oh, those lands, they were also mused upon, appealing,
For knights so bold and pilgrims of ill-feeling,
Pilgrimages to far away, forsaken lands, to ask forgiveness,
Forgiveness for past sins, so rancid and growing of staleness.

And these dungeon passages brought Bernard to reality,
Torches along its length catching his eyes: a lack of purity,
No purity in the lights which brighten the way,
None in the eye of the past, for horror does linger, does stay.

What did the immediate future hold?
Was his guess correct, or was he too bold?
He was a brave man, as brave as any could be,
But felt like pissing himself, in darkness, nothing to see.

A criss-cross affair,
Amidst the stifling air,
A reasonable end could be admitted,
Or horrendous torture mitigated.

The fear of the unknown was knocking so loud,
Upon his consciousness, of which he was normally proud,
The likelihood of pain almost too much, laid upon table,
But bear it he must, for to spit upon the cross was unthinkable.

All four men entered the torture chamber, pain to wed,
Bernard's eyes were immediately filled with dread,
Though no such look fell upon his face,
For he was a player of stakes, held his nerve with grace.

Yes, yes, he was a man known to never panic in a crisis,
As men in the past were calm under pressure, like Moses,
And before him was just that; a crisis born unto the world,
The sights before him so heinously hurled.

These sights thrown him,
So thick in sight, not slim,
To affect the minds of men,
As well as flesh in this den.

This dreaded palace, this room, this storehouse,
This place of contraptions, much unpleasantness to rouse,
Weapons of his gaolers, their weapons of choice,
Those that the inquisition relish so much, in one loud voice.

No matter where he looked the walls were filled with grief,
The floor saturated with those heinous devices with no teeth,
But teeth aren't required to gnaw at a man's nerve,
So prevalent to the torturer's hand these devices, there to serve.

Such an assortment of utensils and devices it boggles the mind,
The depravity of man was easy to see, not hard to find,
And as previously mentioned, despite unpleasant future,
Bernard was no stranger to the hardships of torture.

Oh, God, but here before him this day,
The day poured from carafe a sour grey,
Here was the largest assortment that he had ever seen,
Artifacts both new and old, a torturer's collection, one so keen.

What was before him now,
Wrought heavy thought to brow,
This was a museum of sorts, surely,
A private collection for men of wealth, so burly.

And then the reality hit him hard, as though to stare,
For he could see the blood stains here and there,
He could see where men, women and children,
Had dined with the gaolers: in his head, a witch-like siren.

Then the gaoler gave an order: "Stand there and don't move,"
Bernard was released, he now motionless, nothing to prove,
"Make a sound and you'll be tortured more than you need."
Mmm, stay still or be tortured; upon this he agreed.

Bernard's eyes wandered as the gaoler moved on further,
No matter where he looked he saw the devices of torture,
When he closed his eyes he saw a reminder, something glum,
Much time spent whilst in the hands of Muslim scum.

Yes; those Muslims, that brethren of warmonger,
Who invented a religion from a dream, a dream no stranger,
A religion procured in order to combat the Christian belief,
One to provide Saracen, and others, a little relief.

It was a dream, a religion invented, for them it was best,
To rally the country's troops, to oppose the invading West,
For men were more apt to die for a cause when told of heaven,
To be awarded virgins on death. Yes, a falsehood, this brethren.

"You see the choices I have; don't you?" said gaoler, teasing,
He chuckled, as the others in the room, something amusing,
It was jocularity that they were so accustomed to,
Such a heinous, unforgiving laugh, through and through.

It meant absolutely nothing to them of the expense,
The cost so accosted Bernard, in every real sense,
It was nothing to them that this sack of flesh and bone,
Was to meet with a heinous torture upon table or cold stone.

Bernard was silent. He could feel the wickedness in these men,
He could see that they weren't human, a horrid and evil omen,
No human tortured women and children: is made no sense,
Or torture a knight of honour regardless of guilt or innocence.

The gaoler looked to the others and nodded, more to tell,
He punched Bernard hard: "You keep your tongue well,"
Bernard's stomach unprepared, he doubled over, fell to floor,
"No one said to kneel; now STAND!" be ready for more.

The gaoler pointed out some of his favourite,
Bringing him delight as though food to palate,
So proud he was of what he had,
This man, so happy, so seldom sad.

For it would seem, and now confirmed once and for all,
That this gaoler would also be his torturer, feeling so tall,
"I have a Spanish Tickler, one I know you've heard about,"
The gaoler was looking for fear, searching, trying not to shout.

He was engaging the prisoner's eye, for the terror he did know,
But there, no emotion, he was thwarted, the seed did not grow,
Bernard showed good character in the face of such speech,
He was a true man, not common fodder, not a common leech.

"I can strip you naked, rip the flesh from your body: I know,
I know how, bit by bit, without rendering sweat on brow, "
The gaoler paused, a witless man; moved to another to see,
"And what about this; do you know what it is? ANSWER ME!"

Said Bernard: "An iron box with a concave face,
I don't know that one: never met it, it not yet to embrace."
Mmm, such strength here, possibly not much to be gained,
"I place it on your stomach, after you've been restrained. "

And he waited a little, to see the eyes in Bernard's head click,
To allow the horrors of the unknown, for knowledge to stick,
"Yes; restrained upon the cold of the stone floor," he did grin,
"And place a rat beneath it... to contain it within.

"I then place hot coals on top and continue to feed it heat,
Feeding the surface of the container, much heat to meet,
The rat becomes agitated and starts to dig: this is no lie,
Down to your spine. It can take several hours for you to die."

"Is that what you want, for me to die?" asked Bernard,
One of the two men from behind lashed out, the punch heard,
A fist to the back of the head and Bernard fell to the ground,
Smashing his face upon stone, blood at the nostrils soon found.

Said the gaoler: "But I prefer this contraption myself,"
He moved over to a rack and foot stock on the table, not shelf,
Bernard knew what this was: oh yes, he knew,
And within him a little fear now grew.

It was the sudden rush of cold that coursed through his body,
Yes, he knew, and his body betrayed him then, become shoddy,
"I see the look in your eyes. There's no mistaking what I see."
He nodded to his assistants and Bernard was moved with glee.

With little difficulty he was moved over to the table, the rack,
He was laid down upon it, arms restrained, his future black,
There was no noise but the clanging of chains,
The creaking of wood, the voices in his mind of many pains.

Bernard's feet were thrown into the stock,
Both secured well, he growing over the initial shock,
The gaoler looked at Bernard, smiled, a small stove to greet,
A stove of coals, moved closer towards the soles of his feet.

A little red flame was seen to flicker,
Licking the air with orange-red flames now thicker,
From the coals its heat fed the air, flames of motion,
As they continued their process of slow combustion.

The coals opposite his feet were screened from doing harm,
And whenever the gaoler wished to employ his charm,
To see pain inflicted, he would simply remove the screen,
Gone the protection, and heinous burning would be seen.

"I've witnessed many men have their feet burnt down,
To little more than a stump, to all renown,
Flesh falling away from charred bone, a sightly mess,
You have to submit; you have to confess,"

"I can confess to many things," said Bernard, restrained,
"But some things I can't, little hence gained."
Said the gaoler: "We know what you did in April,
We know that you killed Pope Clement; you, the devil."

So that was it. The pope. He'd heard of the pope's death,
"You're right," said Bernard, "I confess with single breath,
I killed the pope and many others like him,
Just ask and I'll confess, of the fat I'll trim."

The gaoler was stunned, stunned by the reckless confession,
"I see a lie within," said the gaoler, seeing more than illusion,
"Do you think the torture will stop, because of confession?
Do you believe we shall leave, to stop with this intrusion? "

"What need do you have to torture the truth from me,
When the truth has been offered for you to see?
Sentence me to death and be done with it,
For I have a date with Death, and his endless wit."

"Ah; no, no, no. We also know of the Battle of Bannockburn."
"Which is understood," said Bernard: this he could not spurn,
For of all things in life this was his most cherished bravado,
It could not go without embellishment, for all must know.

And he… he was never pretentious,
He never swaggered, always adventurous,
Nevertheless, such legendary action,
Could never go unsung, this not an option.

"So you confess, the weight of such on your shoulder?"
"I do. Scotland has been good to me and my Order."
The gaoler looked up to the top of a stone steps so vacant,
A man stepped out from the shadows, an unknown agent.

Chapter Three

Said the tall man: "I am a member of the French Exchequer,"
Stepping on down the flight of steps, handsome, no leper,
"Would you prefer I speak in French or English?"
Very well spoken, well educated: requesting Bernard's wish?

"Please," said Bernard, "you can continue in French;
I've had enough of the English language, am so drenched,
But I also speak German and Spanish; what do you suggest,
If either should be of aid, and so I wait for your request."

"Ah; a learned man; nothing nobler."
"No; just a survivor; of the world a traveller."
The Frenchman continued down, moved alongside the knight,
He looked Bernard up and down as he laid there in full sight.

"What's your name?" and added, falsely, "stranger."
"Bernard de Beauvais, Knights Templar,"
"I am Guillaume de Blanquefort," said he with a slight grin,
"You do know that being a Templar is a sin."

"So I've been advised; hence my fighting for the Scottish."
"And so is killing a pope, seemingly under duress: anguish."
"He deserved it," was this really about the pope?
Continue to plead guilt: don't spit upon the cross: there is hope.

Guillaume stood over him: "I'm only here to question you,
Killing the pope carries severe punishment, as murders do,
Though, maybe you did it, maybe you did not,
Possibly you are full to the brim with lies, pure-hot."

"I'm going to die regardless of my muttering,
And your inquisition is bent upon more suffering,
You wish the Order to look like devil worshipers, one and all,
They aren't; I'm not; though I shall not argue, nor death stall.

"If a lie will bring death to fall upon me all the more sooner,
So that I can stand beside God in His full glory, no sinner,
Then I wish to plead my guilt,
I desire death, not blood spilt."

Bernard watched, eyes wandering, surveying, a raging storm,
Yes; yes; there was an education about this Guillaume,
It could be seen by the way he walked,
The way he asked… accused; the way he talked.

The way he held himself, so proud,
For all to see, not hidden by shroud,
He was dressed in fine clothing,
Of knowledge, of knowing.

"You can't stand beside God; you have no hope,
That's no reward for murder, for killing the pope,
Also... we are not of the inquisition,
Of that rancid… fraction."

Bernard looked away and saw many chains hanging from pegs,
Arranged upon the dungeon wall: chains for arms and legs,
"So be it. I'll not argue with you."
Bernard needed to think fast, of what to do.

Said Guillaume to Bernard, as there he laid,
"You don't seem to be afraid,
You say you committed this crime, not one of chance,
A crime against the whole of Europe, not just France.

"I could give the order right here and now for it to begin,
Your feet would be burnt slowly away, for me no sin,
I could see to it that the pain you suffer is so great, not brief,
So great that the Spanish Tickler would be a great relief."

The gaoler looked from one to the other, his eager face read,
When the tall man slowly turned to face him and said:
"Go, now; take your two men with you,
Your work here has been done, is through."

"But; my orders," protested the gaoler,
And Guillaume followed up fast without failure,
"If you don't wish to exchange places with this prisoner,
Then I suggest you depart this very moment; all the sooner."

The gaoler turned to his companions, in their faces he saw,
Fear, great fear; and they moved off through the dungeon door,
"And if I hear or see you eavesdropping behind that door,
Then I'll have you all tortured to death, all the more.

"That I promise you. I'll have you tightly strung,
Oh, huh... after I rip out your tongue,
Needless to say I have this power,
From deep down, to the highest tower."

The gaoler and his strongmen wasted not a moment more,
Scurried away like the vermin they were, to avoid the gore,
Not that of Bernard's, but of their own, an unsavoury future,
He tripped over: don't linger, of thoughts don't nurture!

Guillaume waited for the wooden door to close,
A large relief lifted from his shoulders, weight there rose,
And he called upon the others in the shadows above,
Shadows which hid a mystery: but of hate or love?

Guillaume commenced to untie Bernard's bonds,
Leather largely worn, many fronds,
And the three other men moved slowly, but with purpose,
Down into the recess, the torture chamber, walking thus.

They were seemingly unperturbed by this place-of-horror,
This room in which they now stood; this horrid tumour,
Bernard considered: they had seen places like this, frequently,
Or had they visited this one in particular, and most recently.

Bernard sat up and rubbed his wrists tenderly,
Prior to curt introductions being made: disposedly,
Said Guillaume: "Imbert Bonomel, Ricault Michaelensis,
And Johannes Blanke," an introduction, seemingly pointless.

"By the end of this... well-arranged meeting,
We might not be friends, open to greeting,
But we'll know enough of one another, I should hope,
To consider ourselves... fortunate... and you to avoid the rope."

There was hope in his voice, and his voice did raise,
This man Quillaume was as though giving praise,
It wasn't spoken… sincerely, but as though it was custom,
Not even a voice of… interest, but one of loathing; boredom.

Yes; he was a little bored; he held a fear, or was he unsettled,
There was something within, which to subconscious nettled,
He was after... something, and he may not get it: yes, yes,
He held a fear, a fear of wasting his time: he could care less.

There was a small table and several chairs nearer the centre,
Where gaolers watched men tortured; their vision, of spectre,
Said Guillaume: "Let's sit and converse,"
Fast, witless, simple, terse.

They moved over to the small table, the centre of all torture,
Which had upon it five tumblers and a carafe of water,
Unnoticed by Bernard until he sat: not so absurd, really,
Even the gaoler thought these were for he and men so burly.

Yes, these vessels could have been mistaken quite easily,
For Guillaume, and something to tease the prisoner with freely,
Refreshment promised but one that would never pass his lips,
Bernard stepped towards it, upon the wall, knots and whips.

He saw a devilish chair,
Met its unknowing stare,
And many other devices,
Which requested heavy prices.

Yes; the price of blood and pain,
No truth here to really gain,
Just suffering upon adults, flesh and bone,
Did they torture children here too, to hell so thrown?

They must have done, old men and all tiny brat,
But Bernard didn't know the true answer to that,
He knew children were tortured elsewhere,
So why not here? In God 's eyes, how could they dare.

Guillaume had poured four tumblers of water,
Bernard snatched out hastily, a drink before the slaughter,
Grabbing one, drinking its entire contents, the bottom to see,
Mmmm, a helpful and considerate man, thought he.

Guillaume then replenished it and Bernard drank half again,
He pulled the tumbler from his lips, feeling satisfied, not vain,
Both hands wrapped around it, gasping for breath with a shout,
As the water cascaded down his throat, inside and out.

He wiped his chin with the back of his hand,
Feeling victorious, feeling rather grand,
But Guillaume seemed not to notice,
Proceeded as though such was common practise.

"Bernard, my three friends and I wish to question you,
On many subjects; for us it's what we do,
We hope you can shed light upon each, your every thought,
Provide explanation, enlighten us with antidote, not fall short.

"Provide every aspect of your knowledge and understanding,
Answer these questions fully, don't leave us stranding,
Allow every ounce of truth, regardless of what you believe,
Or what truth might bring, regardless of what you perceive.

"Do this and you will not suffer a painful death by torture,
Certainly not here in this dungeon, the gaoler's daughter,
My job is not to see men tortured, for them to be offended,
But to see that France is tended to as it should be tended."

Bernard nodded and decided to test them all by speaking out,
"That seems fair enough; a little honesty to give sprout,
Yes indeed, a little water to quench my thirst,
And a few answers to quench yours, for knowledge to burst."

Bernard simply smiled as Guillaume asked, with no passion:
"Shall we make a start?" was this his usual fashion?
"Please," replied Bernard, "you have my undivided attention."
For he was eager to learn more of this unlikely union.

"I could start by questioning you on the death of the pope,
But won't insult the intelligence of company, to blindly grope,
I'll simply advise that pope Clement died a month after Molay,
And I'm sure this is to your ultimate joy.

"By his side, two small books covered with tanned leather,
Each with an iron lock and containing the rules of the Templar,
Found assertively and with great ease in his bedchamber,
He held high regard for the Templar Order; was no stranger."

Replied Bernard: "As I'm sure the pope did,"
Guillaume: "His true feelings he never denied, never hid,
But do you believe in the call of 1095, the call to duty?
Pope Claremont called for the Saracen end, so evil and dirty.

"To get rid of this world of heathen, once and for all,
Not to allow whither, never to stall,
To act decisively and fast as can be,
For the true religion, for God, held high, easy to see?"

"I do," replied Bernard. Guillaume waited, took a breath,
"Is that it, no extension, no added condiment as though a chef?"
Thought Bernard: That was almost comical in itself,
This man, after a story, something hearty to display on shelf.

"I do believe, with all my heart,
From the beginning, the very start,
For the world to be rid of the Saracen scum,
One and all, not simply some."

Guilluame had a slight smirk upon his face,
A mark of delusion, one of disgrace,
Bernard saw a little sarcasm [possibly] but continued,
Continued with the answering of the questions, no interlude.

"Do you stand by the call for Holy War,
By the Christian states of Europe, all you saw,
To go with arms into the Holy land,
To make a great and noble stand?"

"I do," said Bernard, and not waiting, no need to mention,
Not for a lifting of Guillaume's brow in search for 'extension',
"I too, answered the call, for the great military intervention,
To rescue the poor souls of their demise and starvation.

"To rescue the holy places of Palestine from the filthy hands,
From the grasp of the Mohammedans scouring the lands,
As they clasped their scimitars in foolish effort,
To rid the world of God. Yes; I served; it was a great comfort."

Bernard took another drink of water: "It's good."
"Are you the truc hero you claim to be, or misunderstood,
A misguided fool that represents what was once formidable,
Knights in white; or were you a simple coward, incapable?"

Bernard could hold his tongue and temper,
Had little choice right now but to simmer, to taper,
But this so-called Guillaume was pushing his luck,
Accusing him of cowardice, words so harshly struck.

And his eyes flickered here and there, all around,
He saw other instruments of torture, much variety found,
Those contraptions that could crush a man's fingers and toes,
Another to crush the skull, and furthermore, a vile hose.

A device which could be placed into an orifice,
And then force that orifice open with much malice,
Where a red-hot poker could then be placed within,
To burn the bowels of any poor creature: such a sin.

Said Bernard: "I am not a coward. I served with honour,
Whether dressed in plain clothes or full armour,
And neither have I, at any time in the past,
Ever claimed to be a hero, in its cloak so cast."

But this did not mean that men of good deeds and standing,
Did not feel proud for their accomplishments or branding,
To have that feeling of being honorable but not to display,
For it to be laid for the world to see, as though silver upon tray.

"Being a Knights Templar is to claim such rights, is it not?"
Said Bernard: "That's not how I see it. It's not my ploy or plot,
Any man can be a hero; status isn't issued, not one's right,
Simply because of one's transition from peasant to knight."

"You; a peasant?" Guillaume pondered: peasants, kings,
"Most people I've met, of humble beginnings,
Hide behind a facade: wealth; position: I have no forgiveness,
They don't serve God," answered Bernard in all truthfulness.

"The peasants of this world truly serve God, no other,
Not for personal wealth, not for the fortunes to smother,
They preach to others, that they may feel the love of religion,
They share their beliefs and belongings, this they never ration.

"A wealthy man will turn a beggar away from fire so warm,
For fear of unintentionally inviting many more, a large swarm,
But a poor man will allow one to bed down in his stable,
Despite the fear of a good horse being stolen: with hay if able."

"How is it you can say such a thing, of your sincere thought,
To the front of this court—"
"Court!? Of any sin or injustice I must deny. "
Guillaume was stumped by the harshness of the reply.

Guillaume almost forgot himself: almost forgot his purpose,
"You are here before me this day, thus,
With your skin still intact and not a wound or scar,
None to be seen anywhere upon your body, so far. "

Bernard looked from one to the other and revealed the scars,
Those prevalent upon him, keeping his poor soul behind bars,
He removed his garments so that those before him could see,
The scars of torture across chest and back, a torturer's spree.

And here too, the scars of battle upon his left shoulder,
And down his right thigh, a red fissure-like smoulder,
And the scars upon the soles of his feet, once heated,
Where, as other Templars before him, had been harshly treated.

Guillaume was stumped, but the look of shock quickly faded,
A most temporarily look, soon vanished, invisible, shaded,
And the other three men saw the pain which had been inflicted,
Upon Bernard's flesh: each felt a measure of guilt, unrestricted.

"A story to tell, you might have, but can it be believed,
I can't say," said Guillaume, but for the scars: he still grieved,
Said Bernard: "That's not a question, but I can answer: glory."
He'd learnt to embellish any short reply with colourful story.

Chapter Four

And good memories recall the past,
Just as much as the bad, to the very last,
The episodes of war preceding the fall of Acre were heinous,
So very dirty and extremely disastrous.

The population of Acre at the time of its displacement,
Was 25,000 souls dressed in a variety of raiment,
And 25,000 soldiers: common; siege workers, but heroes all,
All permitted here to stand tall.

A hero was more so for volunteering, upon wall he stayed,
In particular where wages were absent or unpaid,
But there were also the unscrupulous, the lousy, the wretched,
Some were there to take advantage, no opportunity neglected.

Men who served as soldiers, whether siege workers or not,
Quite rarely served without good wage, took gold from pot,
Unless such service was for God,
Only then did they assent and give the nod.

And it is here that we understand their clear thinking,
Understand their consideration of promise most giving,
That entry into heaven would be provided in full,
To each and everyone: and yet so many fled; being such a fool.

The lead up to the fall of Acre was one of turmoil,
A path of destruction and poor politics turning to spoil,
Laying a poor future for this once grand city,
Set in stone was its enmity.

Bernard understood all there was to know of Acre,
For he had lived there many years, to his desire it did cater,
Having served pilgrimages during the journey from Europe,
Across sea and land, to the Holy, bestowed upon them hope.

They journey to places like Acre, with walls so strong,
Each person carrying true conviction, to do no wrong,
As the walls act to protect and do the right thing,
But the Mohammedans bring siege and weapons that sting.

Yes, these Muslim press hard to rid the desert so hot,
From oasis to coastline of Christian presence, for them to rot.
A ballet of to and fro,
Who has the power, they don't really know.

It is in Acre that Bernard found his true purpose amidst action,
But that was in the near future and far from his current station,
And so where do we start? But of course; Tripoli,
Yes, yes; that was the place, a poor place to serve and see.

Bohemond VII had died in the year 1287: month of October,
With his passing went transition of rule to Lucia, his sister,
Who tempted no effort to lay visit upon Tripoli so far away,
Remaining in Italy to the dissatisfied many, there she did stay.

The leaders in the vicinity of Tripoli, saw no good reason,
As to why they should accept this ungodly union,
If Lucia was to remain so far from her given right,
Should she not be awarded the people's spite?

She has blatantly refused this grand position upon podia,
Hence that the position was handed to Sibylla of Armenia,
Who moved to place Bishop Bartholomew, no flower,
The Bishop of Tortosa, into a seat of great power.

Contempt was felt by every Knights Templar,
A cross the face of the known world, il-feelings to stir,
And so Lucia had lost her rule, and the land as it lay,
Dropping it, so nobly handed her, from upon service tray.

A year later, Lucia arrived upon the scene,
To claim Tripoli for her own, a new plate so clean,
To take Tripoli in all its glory,
And here she met her just end to story.

But Tripoli enjoyed, for the most, its newfound rule,
The people here living reasonably well, were no fool,
Lucia's actions from before could not be washed away,
And Genoese warships were there too, there to stay.

Yes, yes; the Genoese, on accepting Tripoli as a trading partner,
Now their protectorate, was in full flavour, and all the sharper,
Were herald to the area to defend it against any incursion,
To prevent troops loyal to Lucia from landing in the region.

No access to piers to city near,
Barred the streets where people sneer,
No unloading orchestrated,
The Genoese never underrated.

The Templars were in no two minds as to their loyalty,
It stood with the Venetians and their royalty,
For the Knights Templar had built much of their naval force,
With the labour of Venetian sweat, efforts they could endorse.

The Templar had harnessed the Venetian ability,
Their expertise in ship building, their methods, their equity,
It all assisted in suit their needs and desire,
From this true conviction they could not retire.

And so there was much tension,
As we can see without cause to mention,
So much trouble in Tripoli, with squabbling and fighting,
Genoese against the Venetians and their impure mixing.

A secret meeting was hence held in Egypt, for Tripoli no pity,
Sultan Kalaun seeing advantage, the disruption in the city,
Saw this as an opportunity not to be missed of the friction,
Wasted no time in planning, putting visions into action.

What good was a vision if not acted upon, when heard the call,
And whether simple, or mindless dreams, you do not stall,
Dreams surreal, or possibly a voice from beyond the grave,
He did not know, but act he must: it was time to be brave.

By March of 1289, seventeen months after Bohemond's death,
There were 10,000 Muslim soldiers, within cities breath,
Venetian and Genoese now forced their differences aside,
But there was always a skirmish or two, ridicule to abide.

Yes, in-house fighting form time to time, none discreet,
Upon the walls and within the city, seen on any street,
Between men not-so-happy with the situation at hand,
Not pleased at all with the situation upon the land.

They quickly squabble occasionally but see to evacuation,
Of the city's treasure being undertaken, little negation,
With the populace placed on board their galleys they sail,
Evacuate in full, tide turning rotten amidst the coming of gale.

As with any other siege, the sounds of battle filled the air,
Kalaun giving the order for immediate assault, limbs to tear,
For he had heard, news divulged in length, nothing short,
Of vast wealth being drawn into the holds of galleys at port.

He wouldn't permit the wealth of Tripoli to escape his grasp,
What was a city when its gold was taken from iron clasp?
Slaves? Yes, yes, there were slaves to be had, many to gain,
But wealth was important, for there was much to maintain.

There was little desire for relics, no loss on which to be weary,
Forget the books and art procured for museums and library,
No; no, of course not; that was ridiculous, nothing so grand,
It was wealth; wealth and position, good standing, and land.

And even for a city worn down by siege,
There was great worth in its future, for being liege,
For what wealth in trade may be lost now or in near future,
Could be won again over time, simply be patient and nurture.

Every country in the world relished trade,
But what if Tripoli were turned to rubble, ashes hence made,
What if every stone was ground to dust amidst ovations?
What if this grand city was torn to its very foundations?

The galleys saw the attack coming, heard people screaming,
Saw the smoke from fires erupt, saw it billowing,
From deep within the city walls, much mayhem and panic,
Like so few had ever seen before, so dire, so manic.

And this was just the beginning of a nightmare to last,
As war drums filled the air with dread; that sound, that blast,
Catapults filled the air with volley after volley of rock,
As well as prisoners and large blocks of stone, much stock.

Yes indeed, all employed as rubble: and a cow appeared,
It seemingly flew through the air, landed upon ground, sheared,
All many of flesh and stone employed to bombard the heathen,
Gifts of sheer terror so freely given.

The galleys fled and the citizens that remained, watched,
And overwhelming weight of fear felt, the evacuation botched,
Fear for themselves, and children, but rarely their neighbour,
The Templar were different, for all populace had their favour.

Bernard looked on: the last of the ships left the port of disaster,
A large rock from a siege weapon missing it by a mere whisker,
A great splash of water surged up, over those nearer the bow,
The sea-faring vessel making good its escape, unspoken avow.

The sound of the battle horns filled his ears, from his rear,
Hardly drowned out by the actions of battle, of growing fear,
Lofty calls from horns for troops to move here and there,
Each formation broke, moved forward, casting their evil stare.

Raoul de Jay and Brian de Gizy looked at Bernard for answer,
Their faces filled with grief, dirty and worn thin, minds sober,
They were brothers, Knights Templar, each one the same,
Fighting for justice, one never to see, amidst this savage game.

"Bernard," said Raoul, hardly lifting his voice,
As though it was too much effort, but not of choice,
For him this day, no sign of panic was displayed,
Only honour and courage and discipline, his life to be laid.

"The Muslim scum have stormed many parts of the wall."
Said Bernard: "It won't be long now, we'll meet their gall."
He stroked his palm against the hilt of his weapon so willed,
A warning to his beloved that blood would soon be spilled.

It shall have a sheath of blood, not leather,
A part of a knight's arm, joined by tether,
Tether of flesh and bone,
Part of his being, to always be known.

Said Bernard: "We'll have to meet them head on, be driven,
Give aid to the citizens of Tripoli where aid can be given,
Be their shield, protectors true,
Until this war is done, until it is through."

"We'll not live through this," said Raoul, "but, by God,
I'm willing for such a cause, govern myself, no need to prod,
And by the grace of God, when I should fall in a heap, a mess,
The gates of heaven will open to me and allow ready access."

"Me, too," added Brian, "I shall want some of that action,
Give me some of that and just reward: to be His minion."
He wished to serve the lord,
With honour and his sword.

Bernard: "We'll do our duty, to Tripoli and to God,"
He looked again out to sea, seeing a fleeing sod,
Not just the fleet of treasure, blood and bone, as some ought,
Making for safety where safety could be sought.

For something quite despicable caught his eye,
Something that stagnated upon his mind, he could not deny,
A despicable action witnessed: "I see before me a sad sight,
I see Marshal de Vanadac and Lucia departing in fright."

"Fear not the sod," said Brian, "De Modaco is still here."
"Ordered us to death, more like," was said unfair,
From a seemingly deflated Raoul, a sour note to persist,
Although nothing further from the truth could exist.

For Raoul was as brave as most other Templar you'd meet,
Would he, though, denounce an order to retreat?
Not if it meant further calamity for the enemy at large,
Not if giving further opportunity, the enemy to charge.

Said Brian: "The treasure has gone, the city is worthless,"
Was their predicament obvious, clear, concise? More or less,
Brian simply wished to highlight the probable outcome of all,
No treasure to net, but the anger of Muslims, to be their thrall.

Bernard looked at them both: "This city is far from worthless,
There are men, women and children, needing our service,
I won't allow myself to watch, see a child put through pains,
Torn from mother's, whilst blood passes through my veins."

The calamity of the city under assault filled their ears,
More so than before; and behind his eyes were hid the tears,
For he did care for the young,
For all of the unsung.

The walls shook, the floor vibrated beneath their feet,
The smell of smoke wafted upon the breeze from every street,
Blown freely about, as though not a care in the world,
And a bird flew past, as it twisted and twirled.

What did a bird know of war and misery,
What was the noise of battle to him, seeming so cheery?
The fires created by war and siege, what were they like,
Likely less than a forest caught on fire by lightning strike.

"Time it is," said Bernard, forcing the play of his mind,
"Time for us to draw our swords, time for the grind,
Time to disappear into the folds of fury that approach,
Time to deal a meagre punishment upon this ugly roach."

"I hear you," said Brian, "shall we fight side-by-side,
Just one last time? On wings of friendship to glide."
"We shall," said Bernard as he drew his sword from sheath,
Stepping briskly towards the street, women screaming beneath.

The three men no longer looked upon the sea,
No longer able to view the galleys flee,
As they make good their escape,
Many women aboard avoiding much rape.

And together they came face-to-face with their foe,
Hand to hand, nose to nose, toe to toe,
Scimitar clanged with sword, parry met by slash,
Stab made against the flesh of an enemy so brash.

The Templars were but few in number, by appearance,
Too few to make a most honourable difference,
A small garrison when compared to what had fled,
To a Knights Templar a battle was a way in which to be fed.

Some citizens would seek mercy,
Mercy from the enemy: such blasphemy,
Mercy they would never receive,
And neither would they meet reprieve.

So their marshal had vacated with Lucia, what did it matter,
To the very core of their souls it did actually shatter,
But so long as the long arm of the contingent did its duty,
All would be fair in the eye's of God, the almighty.

Blood encased the city, everywhere they look, death to be had,
Easily seen was the destruction, the effects of a siege so bad,
A city where plunder and rape was now the order of the day,
One you would not wish to recall, upon your mind to stay.

Muslim men went from door to door and killed the men,
All men they encountered, as though sheep, simple oxen,
They spared half the women, to fill the shackles they carried,
And children old enough to work, to the mines so married.

Brian and Raoul were slaughtered, not within inch, but entire,
Souls lifted gentle to that heavenly gate, that great spire,
Finally the fighting within Bernard came to an end, a flood,
It was by the blurring of eyes, exhaustion, loss of blood.

Bernard was taken prisoner; collapsing after killing many,
Having served his God once more, his destiny,
He'd lost much blood to save the innocent, no man can deny,
He had deep wounds to both his left shoulder and right thigh.

Injuries that would heal with time but leave heinous scars,
Scars which were amassing upon him like a myriad stars,
Scars: the pains of life unless massaged prior to battle,
Prior to strenuous activity as his sword did shatter and rattle.

Rattle bones, shatter nerve, devour men's soul,
All whilst in pain, particular where the weather was foul,
Particularly as old age approached from within the darkness,
This is being honest, being filled with frankness.

This darkness hid many a treacherous thing,
Always there, misery to gift, to readily bring,
Forever unknown until there at your front, as though to nurture,
Unveiling itself as a foregone conclusion: a foregone future.

And so he awoke to find himself lying upon a bench,
He thought he could hear then some speaking, but not French,
His arms were tied back, heavily restrained, so trapped,
Below the rim of that on which he was strapped.

His feet were secured, tied together at the end of the bench,
Hanging ever edge: then a smell thereabouts, a putrid stench,
And it became clear to him that he'd been woken by a splash,
Seawater upon his face, and upon his eyelash.

The stinging of salt upon his shoulder wound made it clear:
Not to mention the taste of salt, to mouth so near,
For several droplets rendered themselves admissible,
Upon upper lip, his flesh: of mind he was becoming able.

Bernard's eyes opened, the daze clearing from his foggy mind,
A sourness falling upon his head, much pain there to find,
The backs of two men could be seen, not far to his front,
He looked around with effort, eyes strained, he let out a grunt.

He was in a darkened room, not much more could be read,
An echo heard from somewhere behind his head,
His eyes flickered again and again, clearing the haze,
He was coming around fully, now able to concentrate his gaze.

The two Muslim men turned simultaneously,
Both speaking in their foreign tongue, naturally,
And then another drew up alongside, seemingly thrilled,
A torturer who was there to see his duty fulfilled.

He was rubbing his hands together for the excitement to come,
For his glory and the glory of Allah, to Bernard a scum,
Ah; and for the glory of Muhammad and his thirteen wives,
He would do his duty, one day to be awarded a grand prize.

"I am, Mohammed," the torturer addressed with a wide grin,
A scar on his cheek, his face dark and sculptured thin,
"I'm going to defeat you; by the heat of my cauldron,
With oil placed upon the soles of your feet; I am your patron.

"I'll see to it you're softened in heart, harden feet real good,
Charring you like burnt meat: I hope this can be understood."
Asked Bernard: "No questions; no search for information?
No pry into my life, my station, no chance for negation?"

Bernard was still feeling the effects from loss of blood,
Blurry in the eye, his gaze coming and going, mind like mud:
Possibly a good thing, considering he was to be tortured well,
Considering he was hence condemned to pain: his hope fell.

"That will come, but first I must have my pleasure,"
Said Mohammed as he commenced to plaster in good measure,
Oil upon the soles of Bernard's feet, to the joy of the other,
The two who looked on and smiled, smiles on faces to smother.

"You enjoy your work, I see," said Bernard, "I see no doubt."
"Save your tongue, Templar, or I'll burn it right out,"
And with that said he removed the small shield,
That between Bernard's feet and flame, skin to be peeled.

Here the burning coals, and the heat radiated out immediately,
So fast was this torturer, eager to be at his work so speedily,
Maybe the torture would be short [but not sweet].
Death incurred haphazardly, death quick to meet.

Bernard's toes moved with the suddenness of the heat,
Before ten breaths were drawn, great discomfort he did meet,
The build-up of heat had commenced to take effect,
The muscles around his face contracted, as though a defect.

He felt his skin burning upon the soles of his feet, undeniable,
And so the screams of pain and torture erupted, nerve unstable,
Screams from within Bernard, the soles of his feet now burnt,
This was a lesson not wished, one you do not wish learnt.

He was within a hair's width of his becoming handicapped,
There as he lay helpless, so heavily strapped,
And the shield was suddenly replaced, for several minutes,
Time in torture turned fast, and Bernard considered his limits.

The door to the room then burst inwards, a man of news, good,
Bernard heard the torturer speaking, but not understood,
"Stop the torture," yelled the appointed keeper, torture to stall,
"I've not yet started; only burnt his skin away is all. "

Mohammed was annoyed by the interruption,
Eager to continue with his work, devoid of intimidation,
Said the keeper: "We've secured ransom. Harm him no further,
By order of the Sultan; keep him well, he's no more to suffer.

Mohammed turned to the sweating form of shattered life,
Bernard felt the world cave in, his life in strife,
Understanding nothing of what was said,
Not even their facial expressions could be easily read.

"You can count your blessings, one and all, if you so please,
For a ransom has been paid for your release...
And just when I was starting to enjoy myself,
But I have work waiting, as though pickings from a shelf."

Chapter Five

Bernard collapsed before his rescuers as they stood there,
Standing before the Sultan's council, amidst their stare,
This was the prisoner-exchange, comrades once more to rejoin,
Little said as man-of-flesh was replaced by purse of gold coin.

Out upon the field, where the desert could be seen,
Stretched out as far as the eye could see, a hazy gleem,
Several dozen other men were moved along,
Carrying their purchases with merriment, though no song.

Bernard was carried away in silence with good aid,
Under the charge of two strong men, volunteers unpaid,
"Give my thanks to the Sultan for his efforts in this exchange,"
Said Guy of the purchased, a purchase he did arrange.

"If it was in my power I'd request the release of all,
Each and every citizen of Tripoli; young, old; short, tall."
The Muslim response: "Give us Acre and you can have them,"
Ah, the price of freedom: Acre the stem, people the blossom.

"I can't currently commit to such an exchange," replied Guy,
To the sour wit of the scum to his front, telling no lie,
"You've already raised Tripoli to the ground,
What would Acre look like in a year, what would be found?"

"What would you have in store for this beloved city?
Much the same, I fear, and no, I am not being witty."
And the response to these feelings, seemingly lamented,
"You'll all feel fear if the Sultan's clemency isn't accepted."

Guy turned to leave but said one more thing to this eminence,
"I leave it to those of importance to seek an audience,
With the Sultan. Anything is possible."
"And possibilities are few; think clear, don't squabble."

Chapter Six

Guillaume stood up and paced across the stone floor,
Before turning with further questions, afore the door,
Walking slow, deliberate, as though in theatre,
Facing Bernard as he sat behind the small table in the centre.

"We're talking about the end of the crusades; every crusade,
The loss of Tripoli and the loss of Acre; so beautifully made,
The crusades appear lost... there seems little point in venting,
As though to venture no further, of desert station no tending.

"So easily given away, Acre given easily; such a stale matter,
As was Tripoli, as though handed over upon a platter,
Why should your story be so boldly believed?
So you have scars upon your body, of which you grieve.

"You've feet that resemble the hide of a rhinoceros or worse,
And the pains that accompany you as though a curse."
And Guillaume lapsed then, to allow Bernard opportunity,
To answer in his way, in his best capacity.

"I can only attest to my efforts by filling your ears with dread,"
Said Bernard, as though from script he read.
Guillaume: "Yes; dread that we see every day of our lives,"
He waved aside the scars; horrible: but he Muslim still thrives.

And that was of importance, of great matter,
For they stabbed at Christianity, as though to shatter,
They didn't wish the cities for glory,
Only to embellish their religious story.

Bernard: "It's for the king and the pope to decide on the fate,
Decide the fate of the crusades, their wellbeing, their state,
It's not for me to question the planned, deliberate withdrawal,
From Tripoli, or Acre; me, a common man. " Ah, most jural.

"A Knight; a Templar," said Guillaume, of bravery no fan,
Possibly a little jealous: "You're not a common man,
No man who wears a red cross possesses a lack in pulsions,
And so I'm faced with the torments of making a few decisions.

"Yes, yes; regardless as to whether I believe you or not...
But you are not a common man, do not speak such rot."
Did Guillaume love their courage, the Templar Order,
Or did he secretly love to see them burn and smoulder.

"I fought to protect all that was Tripoli; its walls, every street,
People, too; I'll fight even harder against all Muslim I meet,
Continued Bernard, "knowing well their ways of torture,
I shall do what I can to protect all of Christianity so mature.

"I don't care whether you believe me or not: so you grapple,
But I care for my service to God and His people. "
He meant every word,
His feeling well stirred.

"Yes; Acre," said Guillaume as he sat back down,
The other men in the room silent and listening, no sour frown,
Each taking note as the question s continued to be thrown,
And for what purpose? for Bernard this was yet to be known.

Guillaume continued: "Of all the crusades into the holy land,
There comes one which was of importance most grand,
And that was when Acre, being surrounded on every side,
Attacked so feverishly by the Mamluks of Egypt as they ride.

" A great calamity it was for all those of the Christian faith,
In the year of our Lord, 1291, to meet their wrath,
Were you there as you claim to have been?
Were you, in body and soul, were you there to be seen?

"Were you present upon the battlefield, the bastions of Acre,
When its wall were smashed of Christian semblance forever,
To flee Syria, the last Christian post, the Latin kingdom lost,
Lost to scimitar-wielding scum, a loss at such great cost?"

"You seem content enough to blame all on me, me in focus,"
Said Bernard, "accusations that fall well short of purpose. "
Said Guillaume: "You gave up the fight, you gave up the city,
Just like the Knights Templar gave up the fight in Tripoli. "

Guillaume was testing Bernard, making him feel sick,
Sick to the stomach, with accusations of cowardice to stick,
Bernard should put this to right,
Bring further into the light.

"Back in Acre, after Tripoli was lost and raised to the ground,
There was a great amount of shock and fear to be found,
It's as though the entire Muslim race had reached out,
Reached out with bare hands, strangled us as we tried to shout.

"Each and every one of the inhabitants of Acre,
Had previously assumed that their trading was made safer,
Safer with the Muslims, being so steadfast and secure,
Safety was purchased to weather the test of time: a veneer.

"But King Hugh felt differently, could not have acted nobler,"
Bernard took another drink of water from his tumbler,
Before placing it back down, as in memory he searches,
"As anxiousness grew within the city streets and churches.

"The king sent a messenger to the pope,
And too, the monarchs of Europe, for hope,
Requesting military aid and protection,
Protection from great calamity as it brewed from stagnation.

"But the request for aid fell upon deaf ears,
As for many calls to action over the years,
And with the lost hope the people of Acre became restless,
Their moods swayed, grew and grew, they were powerless."

Said Guillaume: "And what else did you see, to what extent,
What else do you think we should hear of the predicament,
Of Acre before handed over upon a platter well dished,
For Sultan Kalaun to do with it as he so wished?"

"There was a great quarrel, much fighting amongst them all,
The Guelfs and Ghibellines; Pisans and Genoese; their gall,
All of those wearing a different armour as flesh,
Sought to bring harm upon the other, harm to mesh.

"It was as though the devil himself had risen from the ground,
To swallow up all semblance of society, wherever found,
To swallow up all that was good in men,
Word of mouth was like a sword made from a pen.

"And then came what at first appeared to be a little reprieve,
When twelve thousand mercenary were sent to relieve,
To help maintain order and give protection once more,
To a city in threat of extinction, much security to restore."

Bernard looked down upon the table, took a mouthful of water,
Recalling everything that had happened, all of the slaughter,
He looked up to the chains hanging upon the wall,
Those endowed this cold room, and decided not to stall.

"They were entirely untested, unskilled, an army unfit to be,
Made of Italians with no other option for employment to see,
Peasants who knew not how to employ a hoe, nothing at all,
Let alone employ a sword, carry a shield, defend a wall."

"You were once a peasant, a man of little value,"
Said Guillaume; a statement: an accidental slue,
"I'm not wrong," said Bernard, "some men…
Some peasants are not men: I 'll say this then...

"Some peasants have no skills but squander what they can,
Take from their land, take from their fellow man,
But, I admit, they are not all the same,
Those that work the till, should be fed no shame.

"But I was able to learn,
No lesson did I spurn,
I was taught the value of honesty,
As well as hard work, and this I say with modesty."

Said Guillaume: "I too know of the men, to Acre, so sent,
But find it hard to believe of such unrest, its extent,
How such could be invested by Acre, in the face of evil,
Accepting an untested army of peasants; to die, to shrivel."

"The Venetians had invested much in Acre and were content,
Transporting the army within the holds of their fleet they went,
But had they known what was to fall upon city's every lane,
They would have been more wary," said Bernard of this bane.

He continued: "The army of peasants began to rob the citizens,
The people, the businesses of Acre, taking from all persons,
The merchants of the city losing all they had,
The peasants did as they wished, most vicious and bad.

"They oppressed all those that stepped before them so brave,
There was much chaos and uncertainty, a fearsome wave,
They drank and got drunk, did no work, for them a pleasure,
They spent much time with prostitutes, at their leisure.

"They should have been guarding the street,
Preventing untoward behaviour, it everywhere to meet,
But they did none of this, none at all,
It was almost as dangerous inside, as outside of the wall.

"One morning a huge fight broke out, the treaty lost,
The treaty with the Saracens was shattered, as though tossed,
Flung into the gnawing flames of a burning hit fire,
Doing as they so wished, fulfilling their every desire.

"And so many Muslims were murdered,
The news rolled out to all corners, it thundered,
All had turned for the worse,
There would be no lifting of this curse."

"And why wasn't order restored by the Knights Templar?"
Asked Guillaume of the predicament, this fire as it did flare,
Bernard: "We were vastly outnumbered, what could we do?
Who was to take responsibility, who should act; who?"

"Ah, I see," said Guillaume, "and so you did the same,
As when the Muslim assailed the city, you played their game,
Being outnumbered and with nowhere to go,
You gave up the fight and the city, and this I know."

"When Christian fights Christian, it's hard to pick a side,
I am not a juror; what is injustice: from us it did hide,
It's hard to see unless plainly seen, in plain sight,
It's different, in every respect, no comparison to bight.

"Defending citizens from within a secure location is easy,
Than when twelve thousand are running around freely,
It's like a melee, being surrounded by fights on all side,
Man against man; a free-for-all, of this we should not bide.

"In the end you can only defend yourself as best you can,
Defend yourself against every single man,
Hard it is for one man to fight against ten,
Even if behind a barricade and stuck in a pig's pen.

"It is so much easier for ten men upon a rampart,
To defend against one hundred, even if far a part,
There is safety in numbers, and security to be obtained,
From heavy fortification there is much favour gained."

Guillaume wasn't entirely happy,
With Bernard's response so snappy,
Had more to say,
Prolonging his stay.

"It would seem a miracle then, that the Hospitaller Knights,
Could retain Cyprus and Rhodes, with their heroic fights,
Fights of great deed, splendour from there upon their soil,
Such fledgling lands amidst the sea in turmoil.

"Here they defended against galleys galore,
Denying the Muslims their access as they clawed and tore,
And yet you could not, this thing you could not do,
Even with a great wall to defend your comrades and you."

Guillaume looked to his comrades, saw one of them scribing,
Scribing well, away in his book, a most decent recording,
Records to go back upon as desired,
And back to questioning, no time retired.

"They served – still do – as a barrier to ward off the Muslim,
That expansion of heathen thought, so high and prim,
It disgusts me to the core, but I allow people their right,
But stop the spread we should do, try and restrain its bite.

"It spreads right across the Mediterranean Sea,
As easy as one, two, three,
Yet you sit before us here and claim that such heroic efforts,
A re pittance when compared to your... consorts.

"How are the efforts of the Knights Templar more worthy,
When Acre could not be saved from the filthy,
All you say here, an attempt of reprieve,
All you say, I find it all very hard to believe."

Guillaume was fighting for something,
A bite, or information; clarity to bring,
Bring good understanding to the situation,
Confirming whether or not Bernard was of good creation.

"History doesn't always record the fighting that men do well,"
Said Bernard: "I see your fellow brothers here: I can tell,
They are scribing freely what they hear,
But clarity of vision does not appear.

"Yes, indeed, they are recording all for the prosperity of man,
A jurors conditioning, a scholars, all part of the plan,
But where are such men when there is fighting to be done,
Hiding away somewhere safe, dirty, hard work, always shun. "

Bernard felt as though he had accused them,
But continued on, for these soft-handed.... men,
"There was a riot of the sorts you have never seen before,
Citizens taking sides, fighting against those did once adore.

"Striking against those they considered to be the weakest,
Standing against all of different nationality, as though a pest,
There are many reasons why one chooses to fight,
To stay alongside others regardless of spite.

"Where does this leave us all, but with many dead Muslims,
Littering the streets of Acre a flow the sound of hymns,
Families of the deceased wanted nothing more than revenge,
Looking for justice to be delivered, with motive to challenge.

"Mercenaries are not men, are not brave, not pure,
They are not deserving of the wages they secure,
And nor should the pillages of war be granted,
Which fall to within their dirty grasp so muted.

"You'd be better to equip murderers and thieves with swords,
With shields and knives, tell them to fill their gourds,
Let them help themselves to the sheep and their lamb,
Allow them free access to every pig, every ration of ham.

"It would have been better,
For pilgrim, citizens and settler,
To have kept the peasant army as far away,
To have denied them access to Acre, not allow them to stray."

And Guillaume finished here for the knight,
"Or better still that the Knights Templar did prove to be right,
They should have intervened upon this unwelcomed scourge,
To act upon this misery; this deception, fraud: to act and purge.

"Yes, yes; to purge this pack of wolves,
These scum with lack of resolve,
We all know that Sultan Kalaun requested the guilty,
For them to be handed over as penalty.

"To be interned for the wanton murders they committed,
For murders they had clearly plotted,
Yet the Venetians were opposed to this; we are also aware...
Of the army Kalaun commenced to gather in response so fair.

"Earnest he was, we know this much,
But we are slightly out of touch,
We don't know what action, or actions, the defence did take,
What did the Templar do; what defence took shape? "

Said Bernard: "First and foremost we argued against the guilty,
That they should be turned over for the heinous cruelty,
That those guilty of murdering Muslims should be tried,
But the Venetians were opposed to this, justice denied.

"And the citizens of Acre, too, were opposed,
The argument appeared to be closed,
But I cannot agree with this, despite my good opinion,
This opinion I have of Venetians, of their pitiful reaction.

"The city was large, and news was prone, in conclave to stay,
Citizens in one place did not know of sufferings further away,
Hard to believe, I know, but in Acre this is a reality of life,
As it is with life in Constantinople, one hears of little strife."

Guillaume could see the anguish in Bernard's eyes,
As the knight continued, his heart on his sleeve, no one denies,
"It's hard to protect a city when a city refuses to be defended,
Our Grand Master, de Beaujeu, wished to have this attended.

"He put forward his strategy to try and maintain security,
But the citizens felt we were over-stretching our ability,
Doing nothing more than trying to protect our wealth,
Concerned more for our financial interests, our health."

Bernard scoffed at the thought, thinking it highly ridiculous,
That the citizens of Acre could have been so zealous,
"The citizens looked upon us in scorn,
Possibly some form of poisonous thorn.

"They may as well have accused us outright in an open attack,
Called us cowards to our faces as opposed to behind our back,
Our first step towards the security of Acre was washed aside,
Discarded by the guilty, those citizens having created this tide.

"Those that come together to murder the Muslims at peace,
Citizens of noble city, running common business or apothece,
They said that we had turned our backs upon Christian faith,
In their eyes, as an option for security, we were no longer safe.

"You can't protect those that don't want to be protected,
You cannot argue a point of fact if the point is blunted,
And when a few are outspoken by a vast many, a vast herd,
There is no hope of your voice being carried, for it to be heard.

"De Beaujeu did all he could to warn the Venetians and he saw,
Clearly he recognised the guise of Kalaun: his talon, his claw,
And his army was on the move,
He had much to prove.

"So we requested assistance from the Venetians who turned,
Turned fouly upon us, scolded us, did nought but spurned,
Refusing to support us in our move to defend the citizens,
Our call to defend Acre as a whole from these evil omens.

"I know not if this was due to cowardice or their own interest,
Possibly they were putting their own interest in lights best,
Wealth is a greed of its own, creating its own fear.
And much greed did these mercenaries hold dear."

Said Guillaume: "Yes; the Venetians may have made an error,
But such mistakes shouldn't hold a man hostage forever,
You can see their point, however,
How you should have wharted this terror.

"I've heard you talk of your comrades a lot,
And whether they be considered brothers or not,
It is not for me to prove or disprove,
Of these accusations, they're hard to remove.

"I see the Venetians' point of view, how they felt so sure,
Of the Knights Templar and their failure,
Their inability to correctly furnish and support the holy wars,
But collect your dues you do so easily, as produce from stores.

"You took from the poor peasants of Europe every shred,
Who can no better afford a single loaf of bread,
How can they pay for the services you claim to have provided,
Protection guaranteed, but only to those with purses so loaded.

"Where is such a guarantee now that the walls have crumbled,
Acre having been breached, its poor souls so troubled,
Be they now slaves, or dead and littering the ground,
No matter where you look, everywhere to be found.

"They litter the desert like a sacred mat,
Across desert plains, undulated and flat,
Littering it as flies gorge upon a carcass, appetite to mend,
Covering it as flies cover the excrements of a dog's rear-end?"

Said Bernard in reply: " Yet you see before you the privileges,
From the crusades, having been bestowed, in given stages,
Showered upon you and your king, perpetually to grow,
Upon you, your country, for each and all to come and know.

"Europe has learnt much and prospered from every drop,
Every drop of Templar blood spilt upon desert, on the spot,
Allowed to fall upon the stone blocks of walls defended,
Right across the known world, your wealth amended."

Said Guillaume: "After almost two hundred years,
Of salvation and glorious accomplishment, as it appears,
Acre is given up as though a worthless piece of ground,
Holy land turned over to Muslims, their minds so fogbound.

"The Turks now have a free reign to make good advance,
To Constantinople they can freely race, have their chance,
The Emperor will be soiling his robes due to such poor effort,
For Templar pittance: to save Acre from every wall and fort."

Guillaume stood up and commenced to pace and walk about,
"The crusades were not furnished, simply for profit to sprout,
To see our citizens ground into the soil like forgotten thieves,
Cast into mines as slaves, deserted: each of them grieves.

"But they were cast from the good graces of the pope,
And other great men like him, to give the sinful much hope,
To defeat the Saracen at every turn, upon every stage,
Not for one as yourself to make a good wage..."

"There is always more to the story than can be seen!"
Shouted Bernard, so empowered from within, eager and keen,
"You weren't there; you have only heard stories from others,
And they have heard stories; propaganda inherently smothers.

"Melot Sapheraph, Sultan of Babylon, had gathered a host,
Mighty and surreal, but real and no fabrication or ghost,
And they reached the city of Acre without resistance,
Because of city quarrels, for sake of mere pittance.

"This great army came, to bring us to our knees,
Wasting all the vineyards, cutting down all the fruit trees,
They destroyed all semblance of beauty, as they did shout,
All once lovely thereabouts, left in tatters, no seeds to sprout."

"Did you see the orchards?" asked Guillaume, most keen,
"Did you see it all with your own eyes, this horrid scene?"
"I did," answered Bernard, and saw that they were waiting,
And it was for him to now be accommodating,

"William de Beaujeu, the Master of the Templar, a true knight,
A most wise and very brave, high and mighty man, so bright,
Saw the calamity that was growing before him so unclean,
Feared the fall of the city was at hand, to our efforts de mean.

"It was all due to the quarrels of the citizens as they roared,
He took counsel with his brethren, to have peace restored,
He did this prior to going out to meet with the Sultan,
Side by rank, of sergeant, lieutenant and captain.

"The Sultan was a very special friend of my Master's,
Who wished to ask him if they could do what best matters,
By any means the thing most worthy was the desire for Acre,
To repair the broken truce, he is now the maker and breaker."

Chapter Seven

Bernard rode out with others of the Order,
Riding as though shoulder to shoulder,
To meet with Sultan Kalaun, in the shade of his tent,
A beit al-sha'r, perfect for Sultan and regent.

The measure of pressure placed upon the soles of his feet,
By the stirrups, rather irritating, and discomfort to meet,
Yet, you had to be alive to feel discomfort, and so,
In a strange way, this pain was good, so good to know.

They went unmolested by the many soldiers that stood about,
An army, eating and drinking, prepared for battle no doubt,
They also sat, watching the Templar pass by heroically,
Rather noble in appearance: naive but passing bravely.

They gave a look of… intimidation, loafing, surprise, conflict,
Of the shock of seeing Templar Knights: much to predict,
They ride so casually by, not easily read,
There will be hard fighting ahead.

And Bernard noticed that the army here appeared small,
But the future would change that, more to answer the call,
If these people were nervous, by any degree,
It would not be for long, and it was hard to see.

Heaven forbid what was to become, of the cost, the expense,
But all good men know that once a battle did commence,
That much death would be seen and nerve hence strengthened,
Fear honourably replaced; nerve, an adornment well fashioned.

Was this the faith in God that each and everyone held within,
Or was it God's work alone, being gifted with a grin,
Did God gift courage to men, regardless of God's name,
Muhammad was wise in the creation of his vision, his fame.

Bernard looked around from atop his horse,
As their mounts took them further along this historical course,
Into the concentration of tents further afield,
So few, amongst many, nowhere to hide, no shield.

It wasn't far to the Sultan's tent where parley was held,
Where an exchange of ideas and negotiations were yield,
Offerings enacted, offered between men of opposing armies,
To be confronted by many issues, many eddies.

Bernard could only guess as to what would happen,
And he was seldom wrong or disappointed in all that did ripen,
He had learnt many things over the years,
His time as a Templar had overridden his fears.

He'd learnt many things, yes indeed, much knowledge to find,
One such ability was the reading of a man's mind,
Portrayed by the movement of the body, as though to shout,
A unison of movement and speech forming, truth to sprout.

The six Templars, alongside their leader, dismounted,
Approached the seated Kalaun, a military mind here gifted,
Beside him was an entourage of bodyguards and native girls,
Girls bearing fruit and water, hair, straight, elegant, no curls.

It would seem that not a luxury was missing, here in this tent,
The lines of communication and administration were excellent,
The supply chains must be most worthy, so great it appears,
Such sustenance could see a siege held for many years.

But no great leader of men wished to prolong the inevitable,
How unregrettably costly that would be, economically unstable,
No; a long siege was not justified; siege was not negotiation,
And so it was to be peace, or immediate... destitution.

Kalaun was not fluent in French but he had by his side another,
An interpreter who received no introduction, none on offer,
For he was used by Kalau, primarily and foremost as a tool,
A bright and learned man, who never acted the fool.

And one does not introduce a pet unless that pet is bred to show,
An interpreter is not to be seen, only heard, voice to grow,
It was all so very formal, this greeting, this exchange,
The passing of words, of wide and varied range.

Kalaun got to his feet and moved forward, no time to defer,
Exchanging a hand grip with the Master of the Templar,
A meek smile upon lips, a most friendly character to be sure,
It would be easy to read such a man, of man seemingly pure.

Men of this calibre were never afraid to voice the truth,
A man of this calibre never remained aloof,
Such men almost always listened to another's point of view,
Even if such was to be cast aside in search for another avenue.

Further exchange of welcome and thanks was freely given,
As is the formality of such, no extension of pleasure forbidden,
The six knights in front of the Sultan were then offered water,
And something exotic to eat, much on offer.

William gave his approval as eyes did meet,
All but two knights waved thanks to the offer to eat,
But each freely accepted the water and drank a little,
Before placing the vessels aside, to begin their sprattle.

The mast of the Templar began, of communication well gifted,
Smiles, no preamble: "I wish to see the siege upon Acre lifted,
We all desire nothing more than this, to secure good relations,
For mutual trading, corroboration and respect for religions."

William de Beaujeu continued as he may,
Hoping to secure an end to the armies stay,
"Your men could be expelled, from land by foot, seas by ship,
But the last thing I wish to do is to test our great friendship."

"I'm disappointed that it took such disruption, in the end,
For us to meet again after so long, old friend,"
Said the sultan through the interpreter,
"I too wish to avoid slaughter.

"I, too, wish to see our friendship remain intact,
Of this you can be assured is true, a hard fact,
But to quibble on the size of my army has little conviction,
And thought of withdrawal, shall gather no good traction."

"Yes, it's been a long time," replied William as he did smile,
Thinking, unto himself, of this Sultan, and his army most vile,
Allowing the introductory 'size versus size' be forgotten,
At least for the moment, but he would not be beaten.

"It has indeed, " and then straight the point of the matter,
No delusion, no trickery of art to displace, to foster,
For facts are facts and serve all purpose, sternly and hard,
And with this known the Sultan opened with his ultimate card.

"I'm aware of the situation, of treatment to Muslim tenants,
Of the squabbling that takes place between the inhabitants,
Of their growing nervousness," said the Sultan with grace,
Seemingly wiping clean the smile from Beaujeu's face.

And to this Bernard could see that the Muslims used satire,
Were as free with tongue as they were with their desire,
The desire to spread their religion both far and wide,
Ripping shores of land, the ear nowhere to hide.

Was it possible, the murder within Acre, of Muslim citizens,
Was a good thing; a few spies less, reward hence awakens,
The Venetians were right, no need here to haggle and barter,
Maybe it was they who organised the murders in Acre.

"It grieves us all," said William, looking around at the others,
"But all that can be done, has been done, for we are not seers,
Those responsible for such heinous acts will be tried,
And in this I pledge, for I have not lied. "

But for Kalaun, being tried was not reward enough,
And with his words chosen he was rough and tough,
"Muslims slaughtered, others cast from Acre, lifes shattered:
Many dead: it's misery to me, gone, good lives that mattered.

"But with all that has happened there is still only one thing,
One thing that I really wish for, to take away such a sting,
And that is the city of Acre, to secure it for all Muslims alike,
Hand it over peacefully and I will not strike.

"I'll allow all of its citizens to depart, unarmed of course,
I'm not interested in slaves or slaughter, no evil do I endorse,
It's not for me to kill the innocent from here upon throne,
What sits on Muslim land simply belongs to us and us alone.

"Your presence in this country, is that of an unwarranted guest,
But I shall not allow poor treatment of us in the past to infest,
Infest my mind, position, or decision," and he did smile,
"I accept you made an error in judgement and live in denial."

"Our friendship should be maintained,
For future generations to come, much trade to be gained,
So leave now and be done with all hate,
Leave now before it is too late. "

William replied: "What you ask is much but may be possible,
If given time to honour your request, not turn Acre to rubble,
People find it hard to leave a home well furnished with love,
People are hard to move, but when push comes to shove…

"We shall do all we can, to be rid of war's tether,
But Acre has character, such not worn by another,
In time we shall depart in good measure and form,
We need time to act, in order to avoid the storm. "

The sultan nodded, though none knew if it was in agreement,
With what William had said or simply an acknowledgement,
Did the Sultan fully understand William's position,
And then came the acceptance of notion.

Kalaun offered a counter, to embellish ridicule,
To readily gift the knight in white his final rule,
"I would also insist that a single sequin be paid me,
For every single person within the city to be set free.

"For this you may all go your way,
Go wherever you like, but you can't stay,
Call it a meagre tax of export if you so desire,
But act before time does expire."

"I'll pass the information on," said William, now aware,
Understood his position - he had none: so abusively unfair,
Said the Sultan: "I pray that my terms will be accepted,
My words should not be neglected.

"I'm a generous man, but if my terms aren't met…
Then I'll pluck Acre from my tenacious net,
An army is being gathered on the horizon, a monsoon,
The blood of all in Acre could be on your hands soon."

Could this be, an army on the horizon ready to slice and dice?
This Sultan was informed, organised, so yes; yes… yes thrice,
It was quite reasonable for an army to appear at any moment,
But what the Sultan requested was such a heavy payment.

William nodded, saw the real Sultan, of the fire, the stoker,
And together with his men rode back to the city of Acre,
No sooner was the gate barred, and portcullis lowered,
And William turned to face the men, these he empowered.

"We need to gather the leaders of this great city,
T o pass on the terms offered by Sultan Kalaun, do so politely,
If the terms aren't met then bloodshed will surely flow,
Say nought on the enemies semblance, no fear shall you show.

"Don't release any information on negotiations, of the terms,
Those offered by this Muslim horde, these common worms,
Otherwise they might send representative, not attend: or defer,
I need each leader present to press home the Sultan's offer.

"Bernard, see to it that all leaders are called forth for dining,
Have them attend the castle of the Templars this evening."
"Yes, Master William; immediately, it will be done,"
Complied Bernard, went to his duty, in the shade of the sun.

Chapter Eight

Bernard came to a pause,
All looked up to see the cause,
"So far," said Bernard to Guillaume, "I would pray,
That I served the Order well, would you not say?"

"I won't argue against the fact that you seemed to have served,
In accordance with your Master's wishes, seemingly observed,
But it still doesn't forgive the surrendering of Acre,
It was so much that was fought for... lost forever."

Bernard: "There was no surrender... not in the end."
Guillaume: "Surrender is surrender, all actions follow a trend,
Whether at the initial stages of the siege or later in the song,
Whether late or early: I do not see how I can be wrong.

"Should a Templar change its spots to suit the hour of the day,
As a common feline may its desire, in search of its prey,
To acquire change and need; come, let's be fair,
No, no; the cusp of desire was there.

"Surrender, or loss: to puncture and bleed,
To falsely sow your conviction, this you feed,
You infest the minds of those wishing to take the city,
Your actions, or those of your master, through you, are a pity.

"You did nought to act against the murders,
Deny many truths as around you it thunders,
Lean to surrender Acre at the whim of a battle lost,
This I cannot embellish further, it cannot further be glossed."

Bernard: "The Grand Master did all he could, was stringent,
Under the weight of decision and of all requirement,
My father once had a saying, that two peas cannot share a pod,
But caterpillars and worms must share the same rod.

"There was no room for Christian rule and that or the heathen,
No room at all for both in heaven,
That should not prevent each sharing what Acre had to offer,
In regards to such 'trading', there should be none safer.

"My Master passed on the terms of the sultan, being explicit,
He was exact in all that he passed on, none to illicit,
Including his own views, his own confidence, and confession,
That all persons could depart Acre with all in possession."

"Please, tell us all here today, what happened next? "
Said Guillaume, eager to hear from a lion's mouth, verbal text,
For he'd only read reports, never heard the story spoken,
Had never heard from one so close to the truth, bold and open.

"The Grand Master was labelled a coward by all in the city,
Not just the leaders of those that populated every cavity,
But from all, regardless of the mask they wore on their face,
Here, a harsh land, far from home, far from grace."

A deflating tone raised the brow of those accosting him openly,
Namely the instigator of challenges, Guillaume: so… keenly,
"But I tell you, he only sought to save the lives of all citizens,"
Guillaume: "You sound... tied: the situation, these denizens."

"I'm tired of war and battles, of death and torture so hated,
Of being tried in such a way that no truth will be accepted,
That only unwarranted accusations should be flung my way,
A defiling, putrid plastering, which festers me in every way."

"Tell us; what happened next?" insisted Guillaume, listening,
Seeing Bernard was tired to the core, soft words inspiring,
But continue with his story he must; something was needed,
Needed to be revealed, something needed to be ended,

Yes indeed, something was of the matter, a lesson to be taught,
And Bernard may be the one to give the aid so so rely sought,
Said Bernard: "The people of Acre insulted the Grand Master,
For no good reason: such a pity, a great disaster.

"They insisted that William de Beaujeu had no idea,
None one which he was speaking, that he held inner fear,
That he was concerned for himself, and himself alone,
That he had hidden agendas, and his soul was hard as stone.

"They insisted that the sooner this ransom was paid,
And the gates opened, their arms upon ground so laid,
That all in the ranks of the siege army would hence gather,
And enact great vengeance and kill everyone within Acre."

Said Guillaume: "It sounds like the instigators of this tragedy,
Felt guilty for what they had done, seeking amends, a remedy,
Rallying for the support of others, that they wouldn't be tried,
To be reassured of life, innocence proven, guilt denied."

Bernard looked quizzically at Guillaume: his head then turned,
He saw the look and asked: "That look; am I being spurned?"
"Innocence? If my ears don't deceive me then I would swear,
That you hold no malice towards Muslims, none to spare,"

Said Guillaume: "I'm a religious man but known to some…
To several Muslims that live not so far from me and my home,
They seem good people, but not all can be so-easily accepted,
A vast majority are evil-doers, nothing more, lives wasted."

Said Bernard: "It's how we saw it, plain and clear,
From the citizens themselves we felt no fear,
But I know that, which you do not, that we have none to hide,
Knights are compelled to rally to their Master's side.

"Even when controversy is thick and flowing,
But most of us, if not all, it is in the knowing,
Not only did we wish to stand beside de Beaujeu's decision,
But believed in it wholeheartedly, we held no division."

Bernard watched Guillaume as the exchequer once again sat,
Seemingly intelligent and by no means a prat,
"In the end, all the people needed to do was to pay,
A Venetian penny; a sequin; upon the Sultan to lay.

"William spoke straight: The Sultan would have kept his word,
A statement from Master's mouth, so inherent, clearly heard,
It was said that he was a reasonable man of vast intellect,
And his solemn word he would never neglect.

"Naturally the citizens would also be surrendering their homes,
But they would live, to feel the European cold on their bones,
The vacation of Acre would mean that they would never return,
But life is more precious than brick, it's an easy lesson to learn.

"The Master then preached to others, men and women alike,
In churches and in the squares, that the Sultan would not strike,
And in the light of God within the Church of Saint Cross,
He did all he could to prevent a tragedy built on human loss.

"Yes, yes; He did all he could to prevent catastrophe,
To secure the safety of all within the city, and its holy history,
But still they would not heed his great words of wisdom,
And so they condemned him with words of venom.

"And so the citizens of Acre turned upon him,
Called him a betrayer, some outlandishly prim,
And that such a verdict of guilt,
Should see his blood spilt."

Guillaume: " And so you all stood beside your master,
To encourage surrender, to avoid disaster,
And to the heart of the people you stab, your insult is driven,"
He accused: "To the Muslims, you wish Acre to be given."

Bernard: "We did as honourable men do: applied best effort,
But it was for no good reason, and for no good comfort,
For the sultan died in his tent before hearing of Acre's verdict,
It was so unforeseeable, something none of us could predict."

"Yes," nodded Guillaume for the first time in this exchange,
During the length of question and answer: it looked so strange,
"Please, go on,
Continue with your song."

Bernard did then comply,
Of the truth, no lie,
"Kalaun's brother, Al Ashraf Khalil, wished citizens removed,
With his truest conviction he had much power to be proved.

"Khalil transferred the belief, from surrender to slaughter,
Wished to see blood flow the streets built of brick and mortar,
More siege engines were erected under the skill of engineers,
Scimitars sharpened by blacksmith' s hammer amidst sneers.

"The only good fortune was that winter was approaching fast,
The advancement of Ashraf's army postponed, but not to last,
Postponed until the arrival of Spring,
Only then did they learn what the future was to bring.

"The future had opened up to them, for one and all to see,
The fruits of their undoing, to haunt them in every degree,
The citizens were anxious to find out what was to happen,
What was on the Sultan's mind, what formed, what did ripen?"

Said Guillaume: "And it is here,
Or so it would appear,
That the answer fell upon them,
And there city; much mayhem."

Bernard replied: "It is, for most of all the Knights Templar,
For it was their task to respond, to confer,
And so a single Templar, a Hospitaller, and an Arab translator,
With secretary, of course, we were cast upon trek to slaughter.

"They were to approach the new sultan with many queries,
Regards the possibilities for Acre's future, of military decrees,
Answer arrived by cowardly messenger, of what was to fall,
Seated upon his horse and at the foot of the wall.

"Shortly after the knights had gone to attend their errand,
They had been jailed and then executed: for heaven to ascend,
This was the answer of peace; that no peace was possible,
Not between the Christians and the Muslims, none was viable.

"The people of the city saw clarity, saw approaching disaster,
Huh; so easy for them to sling accusations at the Grand Master,
So quick they are to call him a coward, amidst fervour,
Now they gathered at his door to ask for savour.

"We desired surrender, but the people took it from the slate,
When the tables turned so did their mood, but it was too late,
Siege engines in mass, Muslim men with glistening speers,
The citizenry… we are near the culmination of all their fears.

Chapter Nine

Bernard sat at table, within the safety of the castles many wall,
Again the sound of the siege reverberated through them all,
The walls of Acre were targeted by trebuchet and catapult,
From 160,000 enemies under Ashraf, vast damage the result.

"Did you hear of the Grand Master of the Teutonic Knight?"
A sked Edward, taking a drink from tumbler, a great delight,
At this, their moment's solace, time to fill that inner well,
Prior to taking post, where blood was spilt and many men fell.

"Aye," acknowledged Matthew, "what could he be thinking,
Resigning in the face of the enemy, of heart and its sinking,
Giving up all that he owed his Order, to jump like a frog,
To then run like a coward, tail between legs, a scared dog?"

"It matters little," said Bernard, "the Teutonic are still here,
They have elected a new leader: they will remain ever near."
He looked around the small table at the others that were seated,
"All men doubt, all have sinned, so many inwardly conceited."

"But vacating his responsibility," said Mark, "it's atrocious,
It's completely and utterly odious, impious… noxious."
Bernard: "Knights of the Teutonic need support, our optimism,
They need to hear of encouragement, not of our criticism.

"It is we, the Templar, Hospitaller and Teutonic,
That must come together, to make our stand historic,
We here to defend the walls of Acre, its grime, its grit,
Most importantly the people that live and breath within it."

Said Mark, "I'll defend the miserable bastards,
Despite their cowardice: damn, Contemptuous swineherds,
So free they were, voicing their accusations, a weapon to foin,
Against William de Beaujeu in order to save their coin."

"We need to put all of this behind us," insisted Bernard,
"Whether an upstanding citizen, or a simple… swineherd,
We have Hospitaller Knights, always keen, ready to stand,
To be that rock beside us in times of war, on sea and land."

Added Edward to this: "And also quick to ridicule."
Bernard: "Nevertheless, we are set for battle: battle's the rulc."
"Bernard, Mark!" yelled John as he rushed into the parlour,
Where they were drinking and talking, gaining their favour.

"What is it, John?" questioned a concerned Bernard,
Waiting with slight impatience, to be heard his word,
"The Genoese; they load their ships and prepare for sail,
Leaving security to us that remains: a vicious stab to morale."

Replied Edward: "To us… alone… the city left?
It shouldn't be for us alone to attend; this is despicable reft."
"Nevertheless," said Bernard, "we'll do all we can,
In order to protect Acre and all she holds, to the last man."

"Do the Genoese hold that much spite towards the Venetians,"
Said Matthew: "Depart! They are, one and all, clearly utopians,
And fighting will commence soon enough,
Preparatory has already commenced, it's going to be rough."

"It matters not," said Bernard, "the city's still strong,
Surrounded by a good wall and ten towers, I'm not wrong,
We have the Orders of Teutonic, Hospitaller and others,
And do not forget, your Templar brothers.

"And this isn't the preparatory. It's simply a few machines,
Ensuring they're within range, loosened by blind swines,
It will be a long time before Muslim sets foot within Acre,"
Said Bernard, "but they'll come; sooner or later.

"We're going to be in for a many a sleepless night,
Before this siege begins, by day and burning of candle's light."
Mark: "I saw many siege towers, indicated by a steward. "
"Aye, me too, moving into position no doubt," said Edward.

"The walls and towers are a temporary aid to our security,"
Said John: "With walls breached, people will lose all sanity,
What shall we then then, to defend their souls,
When scaling the walls come these devilish, Muslim ghouls?"

"We'll do a s we can," said Bernard, " give aid to the citizens,
To all of this city, and to God, for all, many a - good reasons,
And the Genoese will be remembered for showing cowardice,
Entirely unjust, unfit: but for now, we must deal good justice."

Chapter Ten

"What did you do?" asked Guillaume, hanging on every word,
"As an individual? As part of the Order? All seems absurd. "
Confirmed Guillaume: "As a whole, as a part of the defence,
Of conviction, emboldened essence, of the fighting cadence."

"Helped maintain security upon the wall, as thin as it was,
We simply maintained a picket within the towers without fuss,
There was be warning enough when the attack finally came,
I thought and knew this, like knowing the rules of a game.

"An Army doesn't bring along such a vast number of catapults;
And then not put them to good use: to strike for better results."
"How many catapults?" asked Guillaume, most keen to hear,
Replied Bernard: "I should think at least sixty: that, or near."

The other men stopped what they were doing; stared; to look,
Exchanged glances: such a ghastly number, the core it shook,
Said Ricault Michaelensis: "I never read that in my reports,
So reverently placed upon my desk, of all and varied sorts."

Looking from Ricault to Guillaume, Bernard said:
"It's the truth, something to be seen, not to simply be read,
The sultan also commenced immediately to dig mines beneath,
Under the city walls like moles, in the hope of delivering grief.

"To have them come crashing down when the supports to each,
Were set alight, hence the walls being ready to breach,
Something needed to be done,
In this time of gloom there was no such word as fun."

"And what did you do?" asked Guillaume for more,
Bernard: "The very first volleys, so thick through air they tore,
The sixth of April, came raining rock, to conviction I swore,
Upon the walls and towers like nothing I'd ever seen before.

"They continued without rest for forty days and forty nights,
One after another, ceaseless, uncaring, no hand-to-hand fights,
I had responsibilities, much to consider, much to think through,
Bringing devastation and depression, and much regret too."

"Regret?" asked Guillaume, looking for a better explanation,
A learned man seeking clearer facts but lacking desperation,
Confirmed Bernard: "The regret felt by those once grinning,
That had caused this great upset at the very beginning.

"Regret for the raucous that was ravaging the city,
The murder of Muslims by the few, those being so… unwitty,
That sought to bring our relationship with Kalaun to an end,
By chastising Muslim citizens: of a life they could not defend.

"Such heinous acts within city streets, upon lives so brittle,
And whether done so deliberately or not matters little,
Here, I say, that thoughtless actions breed a malignant end,
Mindless actions, clouded by poor sense, no hope to amend.

"Fire, stone and arrows filled the sky,
I knew of one knight in particular, and this is no lie,
So honourable in all that he carried out,
Being filled with much grief, grief enough to shout,

"It was when the lance that he carried was consumed,
By dozens of notches created by arrows, as though plumed,
So vast upon his weapon, in the drawing of a single breath,
The air, thick with missiles: still we denied thoughts of death."

"But you remained in place?" prodded Guillaume of further,
Becoming acquainted with Bernard, and efforts of his brother,
Bernard: "There's not much that can be done with cast iron,
A gainst an army of over six hundred thousand, Muslim lion."

"Six... you said that there were one hundred and sixty,"
Said Guillaume, rather smartly,
He needed to hear the end of this battle,
In his minds it did boggle, it did rattle.

"In the ranks, the front ranks, we all did notice,
Those standing ready to carry out their foreseen justice,
One hundred, sixty thousand, many of which we slew,
Prior to the siege turning nasty: give or take a few.

"The army was divided into companies, large, not small,
There was much rest and relaxation for those before the wall,
Ashraf Khalil had a detachment, one hundred thousand, more,
To attend to the resupply duties, ferrying stock from store.

"It seemed that for every soldier we killed,
Everybody that we milled,
Two would take his place,
To refill empty ranks: it was, to them, a race."

Said Guillaume: "And still you stood upon the wall,
Whether crouched or upheld and tall,
Warding off the devil, preventing him from entering the city,
Fighting him from a wall so solidly built, filled with gravity. "

"Yes and no," said Bernard, "the Templar defends well,
I grant you that, but there is more to tell,
We were used to being the attacker, not the defender,
So we set upon taking the war to them, by no means slender."

"Take the war to them!" Guillaume was excited by this,
He needed to learn more, "what a crisis!
Tell us more,
Spare no gore."

Bernard: "You saw the largest scar upon my back,
The length of it: it came from a single hack,
For was not from a torturer, but from a scimitar blade,
I was lucky, my life saved, death, again, to evade."

Chapter Eleven

Bernard sat upon his mount as the others gathered around,
Mounts falling under the command of the knights abound,
Three hundred men, awaiting their opportunity to attack,
To take on the Muslim camp, upon flesh their swords to snack,

They were here to bring much despair,
Not to savour to fresh night air,
And with the afternoon having drawn to a close,
Came an evening, initially smelling like a rose.

Bernard could see all of his friends around him,
But most of all he saw Edward and Matthew, fit and trim,
There was cloud cover above, the moon nowhere to be seen,
The night, darker than they had hoped, but still they were keen.

The Knights Templar held onto their reins,
And the three hundred prepared their many gains,
The gates of St.Lazarus were then opened to the coming affair,
The thunder of three hundred war horses filling the air.

Across the open ground they pressed, on towards the tents,
Onwards towards their enemy on many intents,
But the dark of the night was against them, being so unfair,
As it was their Muslim counterparts, whom rest in their lair.

The night, having been considered a friend,
On this foray into battle, much to amend,
Soon turned against them, one and all,
But press on they did, none did stall.

The tents were reached, no redoubt,
A mass of ropes lying about,
Each pulled taunt, some were loose,
Got tangled with horses legs, and around necks like noose.

Many knights and the horses fell, to reality now woken,
Legs broken, necks broken, spirits broken,
The lights of the camp were not enough to pave their way,
But they fought on, their conviction was steady, it did stay.

The Muslims erupted from the tents with scimitar aloft,
Scimitar to sword, the sound undeniable, upon the air to waft,
Gone now was all surprise,
Muslims had risen, all were now wise.

The advantage of the night, of general assault and slaughter,
Had now turned against the Order,
For there was no longer a single Muslim in slumber,
Each held good faculty and in no mood to be somber.

Melee was engaged, thick and fast,
Much blood being spilled to the very last,
Many screams of death filling the breaches of the air,
Amidst the neighing of horses as their nostrils flare.

There was nothing worse than a dying horse,
One so eager to please, one that served with no remorse,
To be left dying like a scoundrel dog,
Except that of a dying comrade, lost in a thick fog.

Brave men fell to a blood-soaked desert mat as they attack,
And Bernard felt the stinging of a scimitar upon his back,
Being assailed by three men, two of which were to his front,
His timely ending seemed rather real and quite blunt.

He could only make out the semblance of the men's shape,
And with several swinging motions he survived the scrape,
A ballet seeing to it that he could concentrate without fear,
On the scimitar-wielding man to his rear.

Suddenly, from out of nowhere, a rescuer came into view,
Seated high upon the only horse on four legs, his hopes grew,
But the ravenous battle had taken hold of all his senses,
He was restricted to the fight, corralled by its fences.

"Bernard! Bernard," yelled Edward as loudly as he could,
Trying to gain his friend's attention as he knew he should,
He was fighting like a madman, overpowered and strong,
Out of control, of single mind, he could do no wrong.

"Bernard; up here my friend," yelled Edward once more,
Bernard shook the raging battle from his mind, from the chore,
He looked up to the seated form of the Templar upon his horse,
Bernard was pulled to saddle: for Acre was set a new course.

Chapter Twelve

"You turned your back and then ran, to save your own neck,"
Accused Guillaume, or seemingly so; placidly in check,
And to remain calm was his intention,
The word 'coward', no need to mention.

"Would you have done differently? You 're not being fair,
I could have died then and there,
But I lived on, to fight a better battle,
There upon a horse, at the saddle.

"Would it change your opinion of me to consider,
For just a moment, just for a sliver,
I was not in control of the horse: to speak like this brings pain,
That it was Edward, who had hold of the horse's rein?"

Guillaume said: "Would it have, if you had held them?"
Bernard felt as though he couldn't lie; none should stem,
"Probably not; but in the heat of battle... I do not know?"
And so to the wind, a statement he did throw.

Guillaume saw that he had overstepped the bounds of his duty,
And entirely unfair to Bernard, showing false bravado; piety,
He knew he could have done no better,
Was he simply being bitter?

Guillaume: "I didn't mean to accuse you… your ride that night,"
This, his first acknowledgement that Bernard was right,
That he had actually been courageous, had done no wrong,
Was entirely of true conviction, thoroughly strong.

"I meant only... not to shatter—"
"...Meant only to accuse or assume... it doesn't matter,
What matters is that Edward gave his life for me,"
Said Bernard, noticing the men with stares so free.

"Yes, indeed; Edward was pierced by many arrow,
Struck in his front, a few behind, he never to see the morrow,
It was luck and misfortune, each hitting him in the shoulder,
Each missed me by mere whiskers: saved, but none the wiser.

"He died later that night, the truth was real to see, no spectre,
It wasn't until we were safely back behind the walls of Acre,
A long with five other men, staggering back from the mews,
All of whom had been saved, and we heard the news.

"We were told of the massacre to which we'd been subjected,
It was very dark that night, the only thing we had neglected,
Where only a little illumination was gained from camp fires,
And burning torches amidst the Muslim camp of our desires."

Said Guillaume: "It's clear that you were all eager and keen,
But now, your position within the walls must have been...
Shall we say, drastically affected by your loss,
Of so many men and horses, at a single toss?"

"You can say that if you wish,
Almost to the man we did perish,
The loss of manpower, the devastating attack,
But some of the horses we did get back.

"The enemy had them placed upon the catapults,
And they were flung over the walls, with gorish results,
Usually in pieces: a head here, a few legs there,
No descent end for a cherished horse, entirely unfair.

"Some were whole in body though limbless,
Cast as though common rocks, so hapless,
The carcasses would burst open on contact with the ground...
So terrible, the horror on the faces of the children now found."

"It must have been hard to live down; this defeat,
Such harrowing scenes upon a bustling, city street."
Guillaume added: "But better a horse than a man,"
Of such slaughter he was no fan.

"Oh, Templar heads were also delivered, our minds to enthrall,
Sailing through the air and landing behind our Templar wall,
Delivering further calamity and poor feeling,
Amongst the growing desperation and our reeling.

"Hospitallers are accommodating when it came to accusations,
But then again they fared no better, to them no salutations,
On a similar night they too pushed on into the dying light,
To show how an attack should have been carried by night.

"The enemy then lit fires on hearing the sound of the hooves,
Crashing across the open ground, a wave of horse as it moves,
And so the assault was called off, real fast,
But such actions, in memory, never truly last.

"Yes, the heathen scum had learnt a lesson from the past,
So where lies the heroism? Knights Templar, almost to the last,
Were massacred until only a handful returned, totally shocked,
And the Hospitaller; they returned fully stocked.

"So, before you sling accusations of cowardice and surrender,
To fall upon the broad shoulder of the Templar, not slender,
Maybe you should consider what it was that the Teutonic,
And the Hospitaller did during the defence, during the panic.

"Our master did all he could, to give people security of mind,
The Grand Master of the Teutonic had belligerently resigned,
The Hospitaller called off an assault on seeing a little flame,
To me it is all one and the same.

"If you ask me, the Knights Templar that deserves the reward,
Reward of congratulations; to all knights and their steward,
And so, do not point the finger of blame at me,
It is something I do not wish to see."

"If the destruction and calamity was as bad as you say…"
Began Guillaume, "and for their lives I do pray,
Surely it would have been better,
To have brung the people together,"

"On the contrary, they continued to hate and to loath,
Every accusation, every sour look, they were so uncouth,
As the host of thousands slung rock and horse into our domain,
The people remained, for some time, that horrid stain.

"Oh, yes; Acre fell, rather too easily,
The walls, individuals, every family,
Every soldier, sailer, shopkeeper, mason."
Admitted Bernard and then gave good reason.

"Walls grew weaker each day, before the eyes of the peasantry,
Day after day the cracks grew larger in the masonry,
Volley after volley delivering much hatred and catastrophe,
Catapults were ceaseless in their edacity.

"They continued on and on without lapse,
I could see all ready to collapse,
In their deliverance of vengeance, the walls did rattle,
Vengeance manifested incoherently, to end the battle.

"By May the sixteenth one of the ten towers fell to the ground,
Within the great network of our defence, a chink was found,
A gaping hole suddenly appeared to open invitation,
And we commenced to fight in all desperation.

"Should I, here, bestow upon the enemy a little respect?
The enemy swarmed in like ants over the carcass of an insect,
I cannot express it better, it cannot be better worded,
Much was lost, ground that could not be afforded.

"The walls and towers bound the city and now it was falling,
The sultan ordered an attack to take place with much mauling,
And from all sides they attacked simultaneously,
Crazed Muslim invaders penetrating the city most odiously.

"When the first of the sultan's army set foot upon Acre soil,
Citizens continued to fight and condemn, meeting much toil,
Men would run away, leave the defence of a sector to another,
Wiping the hand of responsibility, to help they did not bother.

"Whilst the Muslim scum ravaged the city and castles within,
Men and women withdrew to their own quarter, which is a sin,
Leaving the desperate to fend for themselves in this race,
To ward off the enemy from entering their castle or palace.

"Due to the insanity and ill-feeling amongst the citizens,
It didn't take long for thousands to form from dozens,
To see Muslim invaders take precious hold of each sector,
Storming the breaches, their number too many to ouster.

"Many slaves were taken, many women raped,
Children butchered for no good reason, deplorably draped,
The people of Acre were callous, thinking only of themselves,
Never lifting a finger to help another, such malicious wolves.

"And the peasant army of thousands, so elected to give saviour,
Soon fell out with good favour, a sour note they left to flavour,
And these are the reasons that Acre crumbled, to grit,
Because of the mercenary sent to the city, to protect it.

"Because of the mercenary,
Because of the citizenry,
Each fighting for their own quarter,
And all they meet is slaughter.

"They say a mans' home is his castle,
From where he does battle,
But here we see that the castle is his home,
The city appeared as though cast, a different biome.

"They were rallying to their own cause,
Without thinking, without pause,
To rally by their own flag, their own banner,
Instead of banding together and in good manner.

"They were a disease, spreading from one quarter to another,
People turning into savage beasts, hateful for having no lover,
Promoting their own downfall due to greed and cowardice,
Here we see the simple facts, as each screams a different voice.

"All over the face of Acre did the enemy penetrate,
Like a storm: this palace and that, at a great rate,
They took what they wanted, commencing with a little pillage,
Taking all of Christian value, filled with malice and rage."

Guillaume and the others were drawn to every word spoke,
Enthralled by what had taken place, emotions this did evoke,
A first-hand account as to the true magnitude of the tragedy,
This was a most serious matter, devoid of all parody.

"It was at this time; the Orders within Acre saw the true light,
We saw it all for themselves, without delight but so bright,
That the only way to survive the pestilence of slaughter,
Was to defend what was your own, as though your daughter.

"We did as the others had done, were steadfast in our regard,
And the Templar, Hospitaller and Teutonic fought very hard,
Against the Saracens and all that was thrown our way,
We fought with swords, tooth and nail, many lives to slay.

"And the fighting continued on and on without relent,
Until together, with our followers, we were almost spent,
Every single Teutonic Knight in Acre was dead,
Gone was their castle, their essence, their every thread.

"The enemy had swarmed over the breaches, they had won,
There was no saving the Teutonic, they died; everyone,
They died, rushing into the mass of scimitar-wielding scum,
As they pressed forward their attack, to whatever may come."

Chapter Thirteen

"It was at around this time that the assault did turn,
From Teutonic to Knights Templar, to set us to burn,
Our Grand Master, de Beaujeu, was killed from within our lair,
Skewered by an arrow as thousands filled the stale air.

"The arrows were a cloud so thick, Muslim appetites sated,
Too many to count, too-vast-a-number to be contemplated,
Over the walls arrows flew, no concern for where they landed,
Beaujeu, sword upheld, was hit by a missile, life so yielded. "

Bernard looked from one to the other in seeming astonishment,
They, drawn to every word, his voice an instrument,
And purpose was born of no purpose at all: to lament,
To have this story written, recorded, sealing this moment.

"The arrow found its mark, small partition in armour,
Where the master was unprotected, succumb to the slaughter,
He was killed, but not right away,
And for his soul we did all pray.

"I heard it was a javelin," said Guillaume, softly,
"It matters not!" spat Bernard, justly,
"We urged him to fight, to provide us with courage,
But Death begged of him to give up his rage.

"But he could do no more and was drawn to heaven's light,
Even though he wished to continue with the fight,
Before the sun disappeared that day his life was spent,
Killed by a fatal wound, from the air so eagerly sent."

Guillaume thought then, he was not here to console Bernard,
And so recommenced with his questioning and strong word,
"We heard that the Master was acting more like a coward,
Forever losing ground: no step forward, always backward."

"No, it's not true, and for such heresy... I could tear,
Tear out tongues of all the unworthy, of this I swear,
He had a huge responsibility; and lived for the cause,
He fought, as many, mighty winds, turned into many squalls.

"Our master was filled with so many years of good service,
That courage spilled from within, professional, no novice,
He was one of the strongest men it was my honour,
To have served under, regardless of banner."

Asked Guillaume after a short spell: "What happened next?"
Each of the artisans here recoding that said to text,
"It was then that the Hospitaller quarter was breached, not us,
A Muslim horde stormed a breach in the wall, this... virus.

"They took the battle into their very midst,
Blood to spill, with every sword and fist to fist,
Slaughter upon slaughter filled the air…
You could hear it upon the wind, none to spare.

"Every sound, the metal upon metal: like harvest to miller,
Sword clashing with scimitar and shield against buckler, "
Bernard took a breath, a rest from reflection upon the abysmal,
Seeing it with his own eyes as he spoke the words so dreadful.

"Saint Anthony gate was opened by the enemy from within,
The enemy hurriedly stormed through, wearing a savage grin,
The Hospitaller Grand Master was then wounded...
I'm not sure how, for little was verbally handed.

"I heard later, he wished to fight on, insisted that he remain,
Remain with the others of his Order, regardless of his pain,
But he was forcibly removed, carried away to safety, set free,
Dispatched from Acre via one of their many boats at sea."

Guillaume: "Hard it is, to believe these words, this sprattle,
Each passed on by those that were amidst a battle,
For their memory can be so conflicting, so... tarnished,
More so by their actions: given lustre, well varnished."

Stated Bernard: "You question his heroism, this very day,
If his spirit should hear you condemn him that way,
Then he shall fall upon you before the end of night,
Forget not the fallen, fighting to keep Christian faith alight."

Guillaume: " A report from John de Villiers, at no expense,
Describes in much detail the final hours of the defence,
But nevertheless, it's still tainted with exaggeration of battle,
Lathered in much... noise; excitement, enough to rattle..."

"Death is not exciting," insisted Bernard, "it's heinous,
To the very core it's simply outrageous."
"But still you fight on, " said Guillaume, as he might,
"From one year to the next you fight and fight and fight."

"I'm a soldier, where being cast from a peasant so brittle,
Or a Knights Templar matters little,
I am who I am,
I am but God's lamb."

Said Guillaume: "Indeed, you are that, to the very word."
"What did you read in this report of yours?" asked Bernard,
"That the enemy was so vast in number,
There was no way to count them, awake or in slumber.

"That they swarmed over the dead as a plague, without pause,
A sea of black mist voicing its hatred against a common cause,
That they were driven back three times, prevented their entry,
At great expense; the blood of good men, by every degree."

"Women and children were slaughtered too," added Bernard,
"Not forgetting the lowly, the poorly, the old, knight and bard."
Said Guillaume, not hearing: "The marshal of the Order,
Matthew de Clement was also killed on this day of slaughter.

"Bestowed upon him was much praise,
And comradeship; much to say, much to raise,
But so many also fled the battle in the heat of the sun,
Seeing that the fight could not be won."

Said Bernard: "Not all fled the scene, to retreat to the sea,
Not all in Acre were so quick to give up their fighting spree,
Many brave souls decided to remain behind,
To continue the fight, to continue with the grind.

"They fought to buy time for those that had reached,
The security of the galleys, away from walls so breached,
To the galleys and other ships that awaited them there,
By no degree did we all flee. Even you, in this, can be fair."

Guillaume: "And what do you know of the slaughter so found,
That occurred on the inside of Hospitaller ground?"
Replied Bernard: "Several of their Order came into our arms,
Having been rescued by a handful, having heard the alarms."

Queried Guillaume: "And were you a part of this 'handful'?"
Said Bernard: "No, not I: and the Hospitaller were grateful,
When they fell into our care I was swallowed by emotion,
And they filled with much elation and devotion. "

Chapter Fourteen

The days of fighting in Acre continued on and on,
More so for the Hospitaller than anyone, a great strain upon,
Upon their number: the Saracens had concentrated their hopes,
On that quarter of the city, the crumbling walls and their slopes.

A Hospitaller, Martin, was fighting side by side with brothers,
When walls caved; the hordes came: for booty go the delvers,
A cascade of snarling men in turbans racing to the glory of gold,
For promise of slaves, mindless and mad, not steady nor bold.

Martin looked around and with great sharpness felt the dread,
Seeing what he should not have to see, and so many dead,
The walls were growing thick with the enemy, not ivy,
Steadfast positions upon the wall fell, scared horses at tantivy.

"Flee, flee!" came a voice from the rear,
"Ahhh.... run away," came another, filled with fear,
Cries muffled by the battle's noise, each running from Martin,
Seeking the safety that may be offered by the sea, these cretin.

"No!" yelled Martin, "we have to stay, remain in place,
Do not flee like cowards, do not face this evil with disgrace,
The Lord will give you strength if only you should look."
Those cowardly actions; like a sly fox and fast running crook.

Suddenly a lance fell from heaven,
A malicious wound given,
Martin was struck in the right shoulder,
No further fighting would he be able to render.

"Martin, are you alright,"
Came a voice, that spark of light,
A reasonably calm question from a brother of the arm,
Majestically at ease amidst war, in head no alarm.

Martin looked up into the man's eyes,
"Yes, Peter," he said; upon charity he now relies,
"I'll survive this day,
But here… we must not stay."

"Yes, you are right, we must gather speed this instant,
For the enemy will visit most frequent,
To take what is not theirs, gold and lives lost,
Come, let's be free of this heavy mist, this biting frost."

Martin stood and looked Peter forcibly in the eye,
Filled with courage, no man could deny,
"We can't depart the city, just the quarter,
Our duty will not be done whilst citizens meet slaughter."

"It's finished, Martin," insisted Peter, "there's naught...."
H e turned, sword in his master hand; without second thought,
He parried a strong blow from scimitar, a mighty clash,
Then skewered the man with a double slash.

"The Knights Templar," urged Martin, "they still stand,
And whilst hope remains, so men will together, band."
Said Peter: "It's too far; we cannot escape the reaper."
"Don't let fear stop you, Peter."

Peter paused, smiled, and looked Martin in the eye to say:
" It's words like that that'll lose you your friends someday,"
"Come, old friend, get me to the Templar castle."
And as fast as they could they did hustle and bustle.

Chapter Fifteen

Martin looked up into Bernard's eyes as he laid there,
"That's how it was," he said: a glint in eye, his dusty hair,
"But now... you must get me to my feet, all the more,
So that I can get back to fighting after taking a short tour."

"You're still weak," said Bernard, to this Muslim queller,
Concerned for the well-being of the Hospitaller,
"You're a brave man, Martin, and not an inch do you boast,
Both you and Peter have more courage than most."

"Where is Peter?" asked Martin, looking about,
And the soft words spoken were heard amidst shout,
"He was struck by an arrow as you both came through...
Through our sally port; there was nothing we could do."

Said Martin: "He was the bravest; but at peace he will lay,
He only wished to see me delivered here this day,
He fought and killed a dozen men on our way here,
Courageous, throughout and through, displaying no fear.

"Carrying me, a great weight and burden; I requested aid,
For us to come to you, and with me he stayed,
I pressed him to get me here, to continue with my sworn duty,
To deliver unto God our highest piety: for He, the Almighty."

Bernard: "And there's plenty of duty to perform,
For this war has turned into a blistering storm,
And you'll be sick to death of seeing our red cross,
Our mark upon white tunic; and no time for doss."

Martin: "How does the defence hold?
I am anxious to hear; to be told."
Replied Bernard: "Very well, but for how long, no one knows,
"As for now, I have duties to perform, and the list grows."

Martin needed a little time to mend: "Where is your chapel?"
"Just around the corner, surrounded in rubble, no steeple,
Just after you exit this building," answered Bernard,
And went to lift up his sword, bending forward.

Martin: "I'll make my way there now, return in good stead,
Give prayer to all of those that have fallen, or who have fled,
There are many sergeants, mercenaries and crusaders,
Not to mention the scores of poor lads and common raiders.

And a vast many other civilians have perished this day,
Thankful I am that the wounded and sick were carried away,
Safe they now lay within the boats, protected,
Protected by strong men of heart and well respected.

Respected by the household boys and sergeants alike,
As the Msulims assault our walls, everywhere they strike,
There is no longer a danger for them, just a duty to perform,
To sail for cooler waters, void of death and comfort so warm."

Said Bernard: "We all have a duty to perform,
Moreso now with this raging storm,
But I must go now, continue the grind,
And when you've sought me out, much fighting you'll find."

Chapter Sixteen

"And that was the last I saw of Martin," said Bernard so sad.
"You speak of much valour," said Guillaume, "amidst jihad."
"It was everywhere. Each and every soldier, and sailor,
Many men displayed heart, even the candlestick maker."

"But what of those that fled? The nobles and politicians alike,
The leader of the Swiss, Otto de Grandson, no honour to strike,
With the English army under his banner being loaded so freely,
Onto Venetian vessels, fleeing like scared rabbits so keenly.

"The citizens, so many there were, all fleeing to Cyprus,
What about their souls, where vision of future is their focus?
Are you not disgusted by them and their actions,
Of the leaders, all the high-ranked scion of varied factions?"

"I speak of those loyal to the Christian faith, this very day,"
Said Bernard, "can't speak for all, have nothing further to say,
And no right do I honestly have to condemn or point the finger,
But in my mind I see the conceited, for fortune they linger."

Guillaume: "And what next; what of the Templar defence?"
What of your fight: your life saved was inherited whence,
He was eager for more, a vision upon mind on which to leer,
Lucky he would be, not to forget his reason for being here.

Bernard: "There is much to tell,
Much tragedy and heroics; much life to sell,
But the defence stood strong, none amongst us inept,
All two hundred of us that remained were... except..."

"Yes," urged Guillaume, eager to hear what was to come,
What was to fill such a mystifying pause, as loud as a drum,
This was a theatrical play,
Hard it was, on the seat to stay.

"There was one man, a Knights Templar, of little valour, "
Started Bernard, "who showed, then and there, his true colour,
Roger de Flor commandeered a Templar galley,
Amidst vast catapults as they discharged a monstrous volley.

"He could see the city was falling,
There was no doubt there, none stalling,
He offered men and women safe passage away from Acre,
So long as they could afford such passage: he, a money-maker.

"Anyone with the financial support for such a venture,
Could approach and pay a mighty sum: no haggle, no lecture,
He took huge sums for a place upon his galley to be secured,
Many took the offer, for voyage to safer quarters, easily lured."

"One man in so many," said Guillaume, "that's not bad odds,
Amidst what would be considered so many, soiled sods."
"You surprise me, Guillaume," said Bernard, nothing to hide,
"You seem to be... almost agreeing with me, taking my side."

"I'm a just man," answered Guillaume, man so holy,
"I'm sure he had his reasons to depart so hastily,
Maybe not as good a reason as those that stayed,
Nevertheless... I 'm sure on death he will be graciously laid."

Replied Bernard: "No, no, no. He won't sup in heaven,
Not that I shall care what happens to him, as now, as then,
But you do have to have an appreciation for the situation,
You, Guillaume, do not fully understand the sheer gravitation."

Guillaume: "Tell me. " The more heard, the eager he became,
His interest had never been so heightened, never the same,
Bernard looked around at all of those present, each silent,
Waiting with bated breath to hear more, the story to ferment,

"The air continued to be filled with arrows, no need to store,
And the city began to burn more feverishly than before,
Suddenly the hail of missiles in the air seemed to abate,
A sure signal that, clearly drawn, was our fate.

"The smoke was so thick and widespread,
That in thought it was easy to be mislead,
It was impossible to see from one castle or palace to another,
Every street and field was covered by smoke, they to smother.

"Only when the Saracens were upon their defences,
Did all realise the reality and danger of life's expenses,
They were being breached, and all across Acre castles fell,
Palaces and defences were attacked, to come under hefty spell.

"It was coordinated, very well planned,
Positions became vacated, no longer manned,
Many at the same time, to the core all were shaken,
And other stations were sacked once another had been taken.

"It was only then that the citizens threw aside their citizenship,
Along with all their prejudices, malicious thinning: all to slip,
They banded together, once and for all: but too late is the pity,
But they did fight side by side with others of the city.

"Only now did they fight a s citizens of Acre, as one,
As opposed to citizens of their quarter: with none to shun,
The people came together, to help one another; this was lore,
Something they should have done many weeks before."

Sorrow filled Bernard's eyes: "It was too late now,
Too late to amend; no longer farrow, we were under the plow,
And fire consumed buildings, filling the air with smoke,
Both Christian and Muslim, from all around, began to choke.

"But fire… the land around was so dry, water worse than brine,
Dry as a dog's bone, of tragedy an immortal shrine,
So hot and dry that it drank the spilt blood of adult and child,
As fast as it flowed from their wounds; malicious, not mild.

"Water; scarce it was, yet the sea: rough as you'd ever seen,
At first it was calm, seemingly pleasant and keen,
No sooner did galleys and other boats try an escape,
And God answered with mighty vengeance, no vagrant jape.

"God looked unfavourably upon the deserters, easily found,
A storm came out from nowhere; thousands were drowned,
They were running scared, from a Christian city,
And it was God's city, and so he punished the guilty.

Said Guillaume: "And many thousands did escape,
And lucky they were to avoid a horrible death, horrid rape,
In excess of a hundred thousand made it to Cyprus and beyond,
I know this to be true, for of my reported figures I am fond."

"Which illustrates the number of cowards bred in the city,"
Said Bernard, "Acre, so majestically built, lost of purity,
Acre's defences had been left to those of the three Orders,
The few courageous enough to stand; to die with honours."

"They paid the price," said Guillaume, "but you,
You stayed and fought, on and on, much to do,
And now... you are testament to the sin of those that fled,
I cannot not help but read what is easily read."

Said Bernard, from heart: "It's only testament if it is believed,
For some; we would only go if forcibly... if deceived,
Absconded, taken away by force, amidst protesting cries,"
And he looked deep into Guillaume's eyes.

"Which is the duty of this small... assembly, "
Replied Guillaume, seeing Bernard speak truth, quite visibly,
"To be able to prove or disprove, not to simply guess,
Are you speaking the whole truth, and nothing less?"

"I am," answered Bernard,
Short and simply to the word,
And again the truth of it, all could see,
Truth so clearly seen under scrutiny.

"Will you please continue with your story?"
Asked Ricault Michaelensis, wishing to hear of glory,
Tired of hearing of Muslim power,
Empowered with arrows which, upon heads do shower.

"Yes," said Bernard, "that will be an honour in itself,
I'll endeavour to speak, however, of more than myself,
To allow the Templar, who fought on, better than the average,
Acknowledgement for their sacrifice and great courage.

"To fight,
Not take flight,
To ward off the heathen,
To keep God sacred in heaven.

"I know that almost five hundred fair maidens, dressed so fine,
Ladies and daughters to princes and kings, fled to the shoreline,
To hand their jewels and other embellishments to captains,
The price for a ticket away from death's door and war's stains.

"Gold and all manner of precious stone filled pockets so empty,
Of the men upon their decks, squeezing out every single penny,
As the rich boarded their vessels of the sea,
They paid the price, in order to flee.

"They were so desperate,
Each and every one escaping their fate,
A friend of mine, one of which I have spoken earlier,
Came and said to me after escorting ladies to the pier.

"He said that women of high status were selling themselves,
Giving themselves as wives to men, pickings from shelves,
With a promise to wed with them if only they could be taken,
Taken from Acre, not to linger and be spiritually broken."

Said Guillaume: "I can believe it, I've heard of such women,
Unveiling their chests, lifting their chin,
Being both of noble status or a common damsel,
Offering themselves for the gift of life, but their lives to sell.

"But can anyone blame them, really,
With such purc lack of consciousncss, such folly,
Such mischievous creatures they are,
Under the heavens, every twinkling star.

"It's all such a pity,
But what of the city,
Let's forget the pier, forget the shore,
Go to the walls and tell me more. "

"The Saracens were making their way through every street,
Castle to castle, Palace to palace, Church to church, all to meet,
Killing most they came into contact with; people were slain,
There seemed no end to the slaughter, from causeway to lane.

"There was much gold to be had in the form of slaves,
Better to put flesh to work than to rot in graves,
But the old and the young,
For them there was no more sun.

"Those too old, with nought to invest,
Those still suckling at their mothers' breast,
All were killed on the spot,
Blood to drain, left to rot.

"The Saracen trampled here and there,
Over the fallen, without a care,
Over the corpses that littered the ground,
So vast in number they were easily found.

"I, for one, could not see the cobbled road,
From burning stable to crumbling abode,
So covered in dead,
It fills one with dread.

"The dead were cobbles, gone their laughs,
The dead were the roads and the paths,
The dead received no respect for what they once were,
Men, women, and children, but now with no emotion to stir.

"And the living: not long did they stay,
For they were quickly shackled and taken away,
Forever more, to serve as slaves,
I doubt not, that some cherished the graves."

Asked Guillaume: "How many did you protect in the end?
How many were you able to defend?
He doubted there would be many,
But Bernard gave his testimony.

"There were over seven thousand that came to us,"
Said Bernard, with lack of expression, with lack of fuss,
And he saw Johannes Blanke gasp slightly in disbelief,
Bernard thought then that he was truly believed: such a relief.

"Yes, it's true, pure clarity under good lighting,
We were but two hundred Templars fighting,
Fighting to protect the lives of over seven thousand,
To protect all we could, to make our stand.

"They came to us in droves, into our halls,
Lucky they were to make it to within our walls,
The inner city was lost but our castle still stood,
Stood strong, made of good brick and mortar, not wood.

"Every single one of us that remained did vow to remain,
To stay behind and protect those that feared the stain,
The stain of death, or even worse,
Of slavery and in heinous curse.

"Those that were too poor to buy a ticket away from hell,
Or too ugly to be taken as wife, their bodies unable to sell,
Those with children, inevitably left to us for protection,
Discarded like common garbage, given no last reflection.

"All is true,
Nought you can do,
But as many as you can,
To the very last man."

Asked Guillaume: "How did you feed them,
These precious… God's gem?",
Again all were looking in silence,
To hear more on Acre's defence.

"A good question, one that the Sultan had not considered,
For he could have waited for us to perish, to soils delivered,
All was before him, this siege, in front of his very eyes,
But he was not being very wise.

"After five days of hard fighting,
And more at siege, rather dispiriting,
The Sultan realised that there was little he could do,
Unable to unseat us of conviction, and he knew this to be true.

"Instead of waiting the siege out, he sent to us an envoy,
With words all set to destroy,
To destroy all we were,
Vicious acts from pot to stir.

"He proposed, the lives of all the women and the children,
To spare them all, including the knights and all brethren,
Allow us all to depart the castle with our weapons,
And all we could carry, in pockets and wrapped aprons.

"Ah, too good to refuse: should have been gifted with laughter,
Were we to allow seven thousands to be killed by the scimitar,
Choices we needed to make,
Chances we needed to take.

"What to do, which path was better paved,
Would we become victorious and see them all saved?
We had little choice and so steered away from the graver,
Decided then to offer the sultan our answer."

Said Guillaume, accusingly: "You fell for his treachery."
"I am not an authority, and I plead that most sincerely,
I am but a soldier, ready for peace, and ready to strike,
A crusader sworn to serve the Lord and peasants alike."

Said Guillaume: "The Lord and peasant, one and the same,
That could be considered blasphemous; words so lame."
"You're probably right, and so put me to the sword,
No; all men are seen as equals through the eyes of the Lord.

"No one is above He, seated in heaven,
A part of our psyche, but not woven,
And you wouldn't be so quick to accuse with so little grace,
If you were to see the fright displaced upon every face.

"No, you did not see these things,
I tell you, it all stings,
Of those we protected,
Of all those so seemingly neglected.

"It is true, we were stationed in a castle,
Amidst much hustle and bustle,
Stationed in the strongest part of the city,
Which happened to look over the sea so pretty.

"We were surrounded by good walls, as a castle demands,
But also the enemy in their thousands... tens of thousands,
Acre had been practically burnt to the ground,
With that crackling of flames, that horrible sound.

"All that remained within the city's walls,
Was the Templar castle, its grounds and stalls,
But we had limited stores, and little water,
But lacked not the means to slaughter.

"We were a mischievous bunch, from Europe all round,
Heard the Saracens mining beneath the ground,
And so we commenced to mine ourselves,
One of many resolves.

"Many weeks in the digging, we did all we were bid,
We toppled a tower upon them, killing them where they hid,
A way from the fire and smoke above, forever to stay,
Underground, dead, hidden from view and out of harm's way.

"You must remember that we had an extensive system,
Many underground tunnels, of any castle an emblem,
Mining was easier for us to establish, within system so huge,
The Saracens hence buried alive, in their tunnels of refuge."

Stated Guillaume: "So it was in the face of great defeat,
That the Sultan offered his gift, for surrender to meet."
"And the gift was accepted," said Bernard with a nod,
Accepting the better of two evils, taking bait from the rod.

Chapter Seventeen

Bernard continued with his story, his mind in a tussle,
"And as we all commenced to depart the castle,
Muslims began to molester, women; young boys: so wanton,
Faster than they were able to hoist the banner of the Sultan.

"We were utterly outraged,
Within, became enraged,
By the sour acts performed without a fuss,
Upon those who saw to seek aid from us.

"All were treated in such a bad way,
Dirty, grubby hands and where they lay,
And so we took matters into hand,
Had to, then and there, make a stand.

"Our commander, Peter de Severy, gave command, new laws,
An order to act quickly, and quickly we barred the castle doors,
I drew my weapon from its leather-bound sheath,
Our sudden flurry, causing death, striking like a thief.

"A thief has no commiseration,
And we were in desperation,
Acting fast, as fast as can be,
Muslims began to scurry, began to flee.

"We slaughtered all the Saracen scum we could find within,
Once the Beauseant was hoisted again, I broke out in a grin,
Hoisted up and over the crowd, my feelings flowing so lief,
It was then and there that we condemn ourselves to death."

"But you live," said Guillaume, a sparkle seen in his eye,
"I swore to protect the innocent, not to do this would be a lie,
I took oath as every Templar before me has done,
To fight for right, until duty has been won.

"Our treasurer, Tibauld de Gaudin, was ordered to set sail,
Loaded with the treasure we had stowed, under night's veil,
He took with him as many women and children as possible,
He then sailed for Sidon and safety: of character he was noble,

"The very next day, as the sun peeked over the horizon,
The Sultan sent envoy, vowed to punish, with colours blazen,
Those Saracen that had committed crimes against the weak,
They were guilty, acting poorly; he apologized; was meek.

"De Severy took kindly to these words, this submissive act,
With a handful of knights he decided to meet, to attain fact,
A sojourn with the Sultan once more,
But trouble was met through the open door.

"Once outside and in the open,
When before the walls so heavenly shapen,
They were all butchered, fast; no lapse; no stall,
Beheaded in front of those watching from the wall."

Bernard could see that he had everyone's attention,
"There was to be no compromise of any description,
And so the mining commenced again,
In effort for small victory, to gain.

"When the walls were brought crumbling down,
The sky filled with colour, or greyish-brown,
We took up our arms and rushed the Saracen scum,
Many died over the coming hours, flesh turned to chum.

"And we continued in God's likeness, to revenge the fallen,
Upon us a gift, to protect the citizens, courage had risen,
We were driven to save as many women and children we could,
Retreating to the shore we saved the innocent, as we should.

Said Guillaume: "And so you, Knights Templar, retreated?"
"No, we ran into the breach, under God's eye were greeted,
I was filled with a sense of.... Forboden… I had no fear,
And so with men by my side I brought time for those so dear.

"We managed to provide the escape with time,
But I was captured alive, me in my prime,
And kindness was bestow upon me by citizens of Acre,
A ransom for my life being paid; I, saved from the life taker.

"Children too were provided saviour,
I did accompany them, being such an honour,
Saved from grievous torture,
The source of Muslim culture: his nature."

Said Guillaume: "And so Acre is lost,
I see now the truth, of the overpowering cost,
All that has been recorded, all that has been said,
The Knights Templar were the last in Acre, alive or dead."

"We did all we could do," said Bernard, "and so yes,
We were the last in Acre, the last to die, under duress,
For the citizens, for all that could be saved at a glance,
And what do we receive: accusations from the King of France."

Bernard then drew comparison, as though tied by tether,
"More greed he has than all the Saracen put together,
For he alone has seen to it that the Knights Templar have been,
Wiped from the face of earth, in this he has been overly keen."

Said Guillaume: "You served gallantly, in the face of betrayal."
"And for what?" said Bernard with a linger, of denial,
Yes, he'd achieved much, but his flesh met many starvations,
He served God, he did not seek recognition or congratulations.

"Didn't the pope himself advise us, every wretched soul,
Who spent his days, weeks and years fighting, without carol,
Protecting pilgrims of many cast,
Every single man, down to the very last.

"He gave a promise of benefits both religious and secular,
We, to reap; us who served, in fashion most spectacular,
A promise to all that took part in the crusades and it battles,
Against Mohammedans who rage and plunder, never settles.

"Is this the way in which the Church fostered the crusade?
As a warrior, a man of respect for God, from heaven made,
I was to enjoy forgiveness for all my past sins, as I atone,
Of which there are so few that I can hardly recall a single one.

"If I was to die fighting for my faith I was to be assured,
An immediate entrance to the joys of Paradise fairly measured,
Freed by the Church from paying interest on debts,
Of which I have none, and not a collector to visit with threats.

"I was to be provided assistance by lawful avenue, on request,
To have excommunicated anyone who should dare to molest,
My wife, my child, or my property, and yes, myself,
None of which I possess, for I serve no one but God Himself."

"Yes indeed," agreed Guillaume, as though to forgive,
"But the pope is dead now and only the king does live."
Bernard: " How can the French king think himself so ideal?
What makes him so... thought provokingly and heinously real?

"Through deliverance of character he dispelled the Templar,
When they did all for Europe, he displayed a true distemper?
If not for the men of the crusades, then goodbye to commerce,
For the country would be economically unstable, under a curse.

"I, and men like me, have created a constant demand,
Created transportation needs of supplies, on sea and land,
We encourage the building of ships where none other dares,
Allowing for the promotion and marketing of wares.

"Transport we do, to the East and back to the West,
Products of Mosul, Cairo, Damascus, we are driven to test,
Not to forget Alexandria, and this is just to name a few,
A vast number of seaports: the whole Mediterranean to view.

"We connect the cities; Germany, France, Spain and Portugal,
Once again, just to name a few, every culture from every angle,
Never before has Europe seen the elegance of the orient,
Close up and personal, such an array of varied client.

"So many places, yes indeed,
Prying eyes and fingertips so easily freed,
Into contact with such beauty and elegance,
Such as the silks, tapestries, all at a glance.

"Precious stones, perfumes, spices, pearls, and ivory,
For France and every nation, much economical glory,
Fortunes may be lost, but many are made,
In knowledge we grow too, it never to fade.

"Countries lavish with power, vestibules to a good man's heart,
His heart and mind, and women: you cannot rip them apart,
Great wealth and reputation, all attained through spilt blood,
By the fostering need for crusaders, to come as a flood. "

Guilaume: “But wealth shouldn’t be reason alone,
To consider your position as being justified, as means to hone,
To secure sanctity in commerce within silk purse,
Nor of moral judgements to disperse.

“There is more to life than wealth, saved or spent,
Yet the Templars seemed quite content,
To save what they could of their treasure,
Seeing to it that Peter de Severy departed in good measure.

“Before becoming the new Grand Master, position to marry,
He did depart Acre with all that he could carry,
This, you understand, is not everyone’s... point of view,
But requires airing: it’s something on which to chew.”

Said Bernard: “Especially for the French Exchequer, I’m sure,
Much gold and treasure, bait laid out to lure,
Mmmm… But I say, we have helped stem feudalism,
In such a way that it is good, and avoids much pessimism.

“Thousands upon thousands of knights and barons,
Have mortgaged their lands, no inheritance for sons,
In order to serve their God and the peasants alike,
And, no, no need to say I blaspheme, no need to strike.

“Where rich men of position have died for the cause,
To fight in battle and without a pause,
Their estates have been reverted in ownership to fall,
Within the grasp of the crown, which scavenges all.

"There is no more private warfare between holders of estates,
No feudal conflict to speak of which grates and grates,
Correspondingly, the growth the royal authority has received,
Encouragement through actions of heroism, as well perceived.

"It is to the sacrifice of many that the prominence of kings,
And sacrifice alone, which can attest to this, as it clings,
To their very enrichment, and not to forget of civilization, too,
All because of the things that good men do.

"We see this every day, can be seen all year through,
The artefacts on display across Europe, all to peruse, to view,
The spoils of the East helping to develop various arts,
Inventions and the ways of manufacture, here it starts.

"It all begins with this sacrifice,
A sacrifice, truly not nice,
Where's the greed in that: I do not think for myself,
How can men like me possibly prosper from such wealth?"

Guillaume looked to Johannes Blanke who handed him a stare,
Johannes then spoke, not sternly, and not justifiably fair,
"The script of those within the Order was created,
In order to serve and protect the pilgrims so related.

"And many others like them that undertook the pilgrimage,
Suffering that trek from country to country, to pay homage,
Over many lands of sovereign sway and judgement,
Wrapped in fine clothes or ragged garment.

"But would it not be justifiably enough to say,
That such an Order already existed, warriors whom pray,
The Hospitallers were already suited to provide good aid,
To any seeking redemption from sins performed, poorly made.

"Oh yes, performed in the sight of God: the Lord,
So shouldn't it be said of Knights Templar, carrying sword,
That they were more interested in protecting their own wealth,
Doing all they do for the good of their good health?"

"To protect their wealth!" scoffed Bernard rather loudly,
"Or were they protecting something more, and proudly?"
"And there we have it," said Guillaume, rather fast of mouth,
As though successful in a charade, sounding of youth.

Having succeeded in bringing something of importance,
Out into the open, that instance: or was it simply a nuance,
"You're saying: you were formed to protect an holy 'thing',
From the ever-lasting greed of man: you had no song to sing?"

Bernard: "I believe it no more than I believe your accusations,
Of our interest in wealth and status, they are contradictions,
But it's there for you to compare, to see for yourself,
How accusation can go too far; from carafe to pour il-health.

"There is much jealousy amongst the crowns of Europe,
Enthralled within it they are, from sundown to sunup,
Always in mind, the Templar's wealth and steadfastness,
The wealth the Templar controlled, their sense in business.

"Many wanted to see them dethroned of their position,
Torn from their heights, torn from their most solid union,
To strip them of all their well-earned glory,
Within society and the pages of history.

"To have them seen as something evil and untoward,
Where slanderous rumours spread wild, ill-gotten reward,
Like a common disease, of secret rituals uncivil,
And of Templar's worshipping the devil."

"Nevertheless, such position held by your, I would argue,"
Said Guillaume, "worked towards a financial boom for you."
"And for the crown," stated Bernard, "they were learned men,
Even if transcended from peasants, from city or glen.

"All of the Templars, who had sworn to protect pilgrims,
Of all religions and nationality, regardless of maxims....
Oh yes: A s they travelled across flourishing and barren lands,
To pay homage to their God, in high esteem he so stands.

"In more cases than not, the Templars did this to be...
For forgiveness of sins committed; heaven, one day, to scc,
They had minds to rival others, understanding the politics,
Of situation, location and time, of their countries sour tactics.

"All this, as well as being financially secure and mature,
Being good traders and backed up by their brothers to nurture,
Because they were intelligent enough to fund their ventures,
Should be no reason to sling accusation: hovering vultures."

Guillaume: "Let's go back, just for a moment, to the core,
Your words: 'or is it they were protecting something more',
Some have said that in their trust; in your trust, in your charge,
Was cast the secrets held at bay from the community at large.

"Yes indeed, holding back all, even from those of the cloth,
Not able to be given, not even able to coff,
Preserving vast amounts of sacred knowledge and artefact,
Displaying, sometimes unseen, extreme stealth and wary tact.

"Or be it information on the Temple of Solomon,
Or the Great Pyramid and Atlantis, this great agon,
Or the location of the Holy Grail,
Or the Ark of the Covenant, it being no tale.

"And what about this; the Cross of Christ,
Yes; that for instance, and out holy theist,
We have seen in the Chartres Cathedral, the lowering of veil,
An image of the quest for the Holy Grail."

Chapter Eighteen

Bernard felt then that Guillaume was after something sounder,
Something that he knew nothing about, of something to render,
Said Bernard in reply: "The meaning of the short phrase,
On occasion heard, on which you place such praise.

"The phrase: 'protection of something so sacred, important',
Is shunned by the Hospitaller, in this they are stringent,
An Order you seem to be so fond of, so go speak with them,
Go seek your knowledge, break bud from stem.

"It is the Hospitaller who wished to know,
What-it-was-all-about, in knowledge to grow,
But they were to be disappointed, as was the inquisition,
And within them all grows a venous tension."

"Can you blame any for wanting to know the truth of it all?"
Said Guillaume, "upon all ranks of the Templar to fall,
Was vast knowledge, acceptance, wealth: It grew rapidly,
A true indication of something unsavoury, or even deadly."

Bernard: "I disagree wholeheartedly this day,
On the contrary to what you say,
When noblemen joined our ranks they relinquished,
Their entire property as required and wished.

"The revenues from such were used to purchase weapons,
War-horses, armour; other military supplies, a custom of eons,
Most of the order took vows of poverty, chastity,
Vows too, of obedience, giving up their liberty.

"We served the Lord and the people equally,
People with protection, the Lord with service: most spiritually,
Is it no surprise, then, to all four winds cast,
How the Templar wealth grew so strong and vast?"

Guillaume: "But the Knights Templar, as you must admit,
Were seen to own over nine thousand manors, seen, no limit,
And castles right across the face of Europe,
So far and wide you cannot attend with foot in a horse stirrup.

"Across many nations, and seas so rough,
Upon plateaus and hills, terrain so tough,
Their revenues supporting the largest banking system,
As seen anywhere in the Christian world, no limit, no hem.

"This shouldn't be forgotten."
Said Guillaume, leaving the floor open,
Bernard said: "There is an answer to that, honest and fair,
To which I have no doubt, that you are already aware.

"King Philip convinced Pope Clement, calmly told,
That the Templar as a whole were not bold,
Not supporters of their Holy faith,
But the devils in disguise, powerfully unsafe.

"He advised that the Templar were looking to destroy,
Take the religion apart, an heavenous ploy,
King Philip of France wanted for them all to be persecuted,
Wanting their financial and political power cleanly muted.

"It was then that the pope gave orders,
For an inquisition to begin, with multiple murders,
Right across France the Templar were taken, put under arrest,
Taken to be convicted by ridiculous measure, of this I attest.

Said Guillaume: "But many fled, before noon's bell,
Including the naval force which was anchored in La Rochelle."
Bernard: "Can you blame them: all on land were arrested,
They were tried, found guilty; shameful conviction invested.

"It would have been the same for those anchored near shores,
On the piers of La Rochelle, with all of their stores."
Guillaume: "Let us pause, just for a moment, have a rest,
Have a drink, Bernard; quench your thirst, be my guest."

Bernard took a drink and leaned back a little,
Prepared himself mentally for the coming battle,
Looking again into the eyes of all those seated around,
Each taking notes, or reading them, without a sound.

Guillaume then did recommence, a feeling of solace to sow,
"My job today, is not to find you guilty... guilty; no,
I am simply here to find out more about you,
To get down to the truth of your life; all you did and do."

Bernard: "And why should my life be so important?
Is it not something you can say, to give, to grant?"
Guillaume: " They say you killed the pope, in times so rough,
None of us here believes in your guilt, but belief isn't enough."

Bernard was stumped: where was this leading, what was it for,
"Are you concerned the Templar shall be seen without a fetor?
Or is it the king who's afraid of giving them power... position,
Giving them the opposite of what he wishes, to be a lesion?"

"When your master was burnt as the stake he gave notice,
That the pope and the king would fall; spoken in strong voice."
"The king is concerned for his safety?" was Bernard's reply,
"Shouldn't he be?" asked Guillaume: on what could he rely?

"I assume there must be many men hoping to cross that moat,
Get their grubby little hands around the king's throat."
Said Bernard: " Including the French Exchequer. "
Receiving a sudden stare from all, each able to be the avenger.

"No one is without good reason," said Guillaume, most calm,
"But you are seen as a threat, I am not," did that ring alarm?
"Let's move on to the trial in Cyprus," said Imbert, impatient,
"A change of note may promote calm; so let us reorient."

"Possibly," said Bernard, "but then again,
Maybe you have a hidden agenda, not yet made plain."
Guillaume: "Let's begin; one hundred twenty six questions,
Asked of witnesses to the Templars' behaviour; their notions.

"Men like James of Plany; Rupen of Montfort; and Percival,
Lord of Mar included, each offering their disapproval,
It is said that the Knights Templar were offered freedom,
By the Egyptian Sultan, if they would deny God, his kingdom.

"In what would seem to be true Templar fashion at play,
As in accordance with what you have been saying this day,
They refused to deny the Christian faith, in single breath,
Each and every knight captured was willing to be put to death.

"These three men and many others like them, rigid as iron rod,
Would rather die in putrid condition than deny their God,
Happy to be decapitated as opposed to denying Jesus Christ,
Christ their savour, each man believing, not one a deist.

"They were then refused access to food and water,
Their gaolers locked them away to perish, no need to slaughter,
Such strength in men proves that the Knights Templar,
Would not go against their belief, held lofty by a strong pillar.

"But the inquisition saw to it that many confessed,
In their manipulation they were blessed,
Putting each man to the test,
Where they denied Christ at their best."

Said Bernard: "In the face of torture,"
"Yes," agreed Guillaume, "in the face of painful lecture,
Just as you, yourself, have admitted to killing the pope,
In the face of torture, to receive reprieve is your hope."

Said Bernard: "Death by starvation is easier to handle,"
"How do you know?" asked Guillaume, "was it the infidel?"
"Mmmm… call it a guess... I've been tortured in the past,
There is no room for dying with dignity, none that will last.

"When tortured to death, you scream out denials,
Said Bernard, "such voice is commanded, and it defiles,
It stains all you know of past, present and future,
No knowledge is stable, there's none to nurture."

"Others, also, swear to the heroism of many a strong knight,"
Continued Guillaume, amidst flicker of candle and torch light,
"Take for example Thomas, Lord of Pingueno, what he said,
He witnessed many decapitations, no denials there wed."

"A quick death is a good death when on the battlefield,"
Said Bernard, "it's very merciful, no satisfaction to yield."
Guillaume was sorry for Bernard and his predicament,
Was sorry for… taking advantage, to use him as an instrument.

"Balian, Lord of Montgisard; Marshal of Cyprus,
Ayme of Osilliers; and others like them, without fuss,
Swore that the Templars were noble warriors and bold,
Of their vows to chastity and obedience, they did uphold.

"And above all, that they possessed no idols,
But had good morals,
Even bishops have said that the Knights Templar believed,
In the sacraments of the altar, from this, love they received.

"It seems to me, therefore, in the face of so many witnesses,
Assessing all question and answer, not looking at wild guesses,
Seeing all that you are, as an Order, seeing all the hidden facts,
Are incapable of blasphemous and sacrilegious acts."

"Thank you," said Bernard, a small grin, but had he won?
"It seems that your task here is well and truly done."
"On the contrary, I still have much I wish to discuss with you,"
Said Guillaume, adding, "we are far, far from being through."

"I'm growing tired," said Bernard, not in the mood,
"It's not easy, locked away in a dungeon with little to no food,
The water helps, and the bliss it provides is no stranger,
But it doesn't serve to take away my hunger."

"I have no food," said Guillaume, "I have none about,
Nor am I about to disrupt this meeting of ours, so do not pout,
We have done so well: w e'll continue until we're done,
Then, and only then, you can tear into bread, have your fun."

"Very well," said Bernard, "let the water do its trick,
And let's get the questioning over with, nice and quick."
"Thank you," said Guillaume, preparing himself for the task,
Of asking more questions: sole purpose hidden behind mask.

Chapter Nineteen

"John Balliol, crowned King of Scotland at Scone in 1292,"
Said Guillaume, Bernard interjecting before he was through,
"What does this have to do with the pope?" asked Bernard,
"It is necessary," said Guillaume, "allow me to go forward."

"Very well," said Bernard, guilt forming, a strong image,
"...Scone in 1292... in April of 1296 he renounced homage,
Renouncing Edward, King of England, insult to stick,
King Edward then invaded Scotland and sacked Berwick.

"The Battle of Dunbar then followed, to his rapture,
And Edinburgh castle he did capture,
On the tenth of July, Balliol abdicated, was exiled to France,
Scottish rebellion ensued, William Wallace taking firm stance.

"The Bridge of Stirling, the English, beaten where they stand,
And Wallace led his men over the border into Northumberland,
Where they plundered and burned wherever they went,
Revenge for what was done in Scotland, anger hence vent."

"I'm sure this must be leading somewhere," said Bernard,
Awaiting to hear of further word,
Shallow guilt seen to appear upon his face,
Discomfort here but no disgrace.

"In 1298, the Battle of Falkirk, Wallace defeated at the fight,
Wallace was executed in 1305, and i n 1306 comes a light,
Robert the Bruce is hence crowned King of Scotland,
Coming of power, moved against the Brits, made a stand.

"In 1306 the pope sees Robert the Bruce excommunicated,
A year prior to persecution of Templar being disseminated,
Gifted here, future salvation to come, to Templar from north,
Robert the Bruce decreeing dissemination of little worth.

"On the morning of Friday the thirteenth of October, 1307,
Right across the face of France, in full view of heaven,
Most of the Templar Knights were captured, put into chains,
To suffer mortal wounds, indicted, to receive a variety of pains.

"The knights were tortured, and propaganda was in full swing,
A letter dated December twenty-fourth, 1310, prior to Spring,
Was dispatched to England, from the papacy,
A decisive effort to have arrested the Templars for heresy.

"In England it was received poorly, in it nothing to invest,
King Edward the Second delaying this order to arrest,
But eventually the Templar were drawn to questioning,
Byt unfavourable means and with little warning.

"Torture was introduced to the English legal system, it tested,
And anyone giving aid to the Templars were also arrested,
A vast many people were excommunicated, suitably punished,
Templars given a year to turn themselves in: many vanished.

"The King of England happily seized Templar lands and assets,
Depriving them of necessary support, disregarding their tenets,
Scotland therefore became a beacon for the Templar cause,
It was to become a safe haven for them all, of influx no pause."

"Why would they,
With such a law: a decree: stay,
Aid the Templar they would,
As they felt they should.

"No effort at all was ever made to prosecute the Knighthood,
Not there, at the heights of Scotland, where the Bruce stood,
Such a major attraction it was to many Templars in hiding,
Not openly calling themselves Templar as they went riding.

"They continued to exercise power within the world,
Again armour worn and all wielding a sword and shield,
When Edward died in 1307, enroute to Scotland and battle,
So went sovereignty to a weaker son, a man so brittle.

"And with the death and transfer of power,
Came a limited peace, a light shower,
In effect, to simmer, never at the boil,
Never true battle, never brutal trouble or toil.".

Guillaume put down the paper in his hand,
"And then the rain poured, cast all over the land,
Robert the Bruce laid siege to Stirling Castle and won,
A year later Edward led an army under the warmth of the sun.

"Edward came to Scotland with an army of Welsh and English,
With Gascons from Aquitaine, victory being his only wish,
Robert was a capable general, Edward the Second was not,
The year is 1314, June. What can you tell me of this lot?"

Asked Bernard; "What... what am I supposed to say?"
Guillaume: "I want to know your part in this play,
I have reports on the information of your earlier questioning,
I simply wish the truth; your investment against this king."

"Do you wish me to boast of my courage, none to deprive,
Or simply advise of my efforts to remain alive?"
"Your story, as you see it," answered Guillaume, his last word,
Waiting patiently now for a story to be heard.

Chapter Twenty

"Scotland has suffered at the hands of this English savage,"
Said Robert the Bruce, "he'll reap what's sown, is the adage,
Damn filthy swine they are,
From county and country so far.

"Service; service to God and country is what I owe,
Service to the people of this grand land I shall sow,"
Robert paced the floor and turned abruptly,
To face Bernard square in the face, rather aptly.

"Your assistance in this matter is greatly appreciated,
More so than I can possibly express, not overrated,
The English will piss their pants when they see you coming,
Over the rise…. Hah; their mouths with rage frothing.

"Yes; you there, charging their ranks at full speed,
Into the mouth of battle, a fight you badly need,
Banners flying high above, your swords to slash, ready to lay,
The wind catching the grace of that which you shall display."

"You have served us," said Bernard truthfully,
"We simply repay the favour, and for God's glory."
The Bruce: "From ships and land you have flocked,
Into our arms, t o rally at our side and fully stocked.

"You come here, in this, our time of need,
You have no hidden agenda, no greed,
You, and I, shall not be beaten,
You will not be forgotten."

Voiced Bernard: "That, my friend, will always be doubted,
"Wheels are in motion, but our stand here will go unrecorded,
The French king will see to it that we are banished,
Stricken from the books of history as he sorely has wished.

"Where it is within his power to do so,
All tracks of our service will be buried beneath a heavy snow,
So cowardly he hides behind the English, he does it well,
When the fight is done, the Templar shall be an empty well."

"Don't speak so," insisted Robert, "such a foul stench,
Such words should serve to denounce the English or French,
But not good men as you and your brethren,
Not of your Order and all of its children.

"Many people see you as renegades, but I see much more,
I see honour in your eyes, courage, you are honest to the core,
Edward's armies have harried us for too long, filled with hate,
And now it is time for us to set the record straight."

Said Bernard: “If you fail, you’ll surely die,
Just like William Wallace, who lived, eye for eye.”
“He died with honour; I can die like that too,
But to live; aye; we must all live, see this through.

“Yes, the answer, fight like we’ve never fought before,
Fight with all we have, nought left in store,
If we fail then Scotland be damned, we lose our kingdom,
But victory will secure all we ask, give us our freedom.”

“How many fights must you win before freedom is secured,
How many battles; and can the English be lured?”
Robert: “Yes they can, just this one time, and the time is near,
Freedom in reach; yes, yes; time in nigh to release their fear.”

Robert sat back down opposite Bernard,
Both took a drink of their tumbler, their third,
Alone they were, to speak freely on the coming battle,
As the wind outside hit and the shutters did rattle.

Said Robert: “They aren’t far from here, I smell them already.”
Spoken with a detested smile upon face, rock steady,
“We shall make a mockery of them, tooth and nail,
We shall take the fight to them when ripe, we shall not fail.”

Bernard: “Aye, I know it, for only knowledge can be obtained,
Obtained from your courageous words, varnished, unstained,
And what is the latest report on this English tide,
This one that comes at full gallop, at a fast ride?”

Said Robert: "The same, they out number us in arms and men,
In both armour and horse; hah, scurrying like pigs from pen,
They hunger for something but know not what,
But we have cadence and direction amongst our lot.

"They are twenty thousand and we are but six: all with heart,
They have three thousand mounted, we; five hundred to start,"
Robert shook it from his mind: "We are on the eve of battle,
Do you have all you need, before I continue my brattle?"

"With six thousand Scots ready to fight and die, by and large,
Templars with mounts ready to enact a surprise charge,
We need little else but gravediggers to prepare their bed,
And thousands of labourers to then bury their dead."

Robert slapped him on the back,
"Hah! let the crows have their snack."
The door suddenly burst open and a man hurried through,
A squire securing it fast against the cold, as one would do.

Robert looked at the man, lifting his eyebrows,
As a common farmer may look upon his cows,
Recognising who it was he suddenly became pleased,
Light of open fire illuminating the man, concerns eased.

Robert was upon his feet and smiling,
In this there was no denying,
Bernard also stood, seeing that familiarity was present,
Seeing the smiles presented by both, a simile, of consent.

"Bernard, this good man is the one and only, Alexander Seton."
Good friendship appeared to hold, no doubt with good reason,
Bernard knew that Seton was a Templar, too,
And bestowed greeting upon him as one would do.

Alexander: "I came as soon as I could. The English are here."
Robert: "My report gives their number twenty thousand."
"Add three thousand more and the number will be closer, "
Said Alexander, "closer to the truth, for my spy is a master. "

Seton looked at Bernard: "A surcoat with a red cross,
How many men are we, what is our gross?"
"Our? We? " said Bernard with a smile and short laugh,
Unfurling from around his neck a ragged tartan cloth, his scarf.

Alexander: "You don't expect me to stand by and watch,
You having your fun, me sitting back, no kill to notch?"
Robert: "Always spoiling for a fight,
When not engaged in one: am I not right?"

"Help it not for it is within my ancestry,
Whether noble or from peasantry,
My father and relative, John, look forward to joining rank,
As I do in joining the Knights Templar, not to sit on the bank."

"It would be an honour," said Bernard, "I humbly accept,
Your voluntary assistance is commendable, far from inept,
Bernard looked to Robert and back, this grand unity,
"It appears that we now number, exactly, sixty."

Said Alexander; "Hmm, I'd say fifty more than we need."
"I believe every word of it," said Robert, "we are all agreed,
We also have secured the Sinclair's, and Sir Adam Gordon,
And, of course, his associates, along with their guidon."

Said Alexander as he laughed: "So I've found good company,
We few, amongst the many."
And he pulled up a chair,
All were content, all seemed fair.

Chapter Twenty-One

June 24th, 1314. Bannockburn was a site to see,
Six thousand Scots standing ground, never to flee,
Opposing more than twenty thousand, there on the spot,
An army to put fear into any man, except a Scot.

The armies were two and a half miles from Stirling castle,
At Bannockburn, this, their field of battle,
The Scottish army was made up of almost all foot, but sturdy,
Armed with spears, battle axes and pikes, not ragged or untidy.

Dressed in an array of colour,
Tartans of varied flavour,
Faces adorned with paint and fanfare,
Looked upon by an English cold stare.

The mounted men carried the swords of Scottish legend,
Here to front all savagery, here to defend, to the end,
They wished to unseat the nerves of the foe,
But the English nerve was steadfast, in this they know.

They know because of intelligence,
No scruples inhibit action, none to fence,
For it was a simple affair, one you could see in slumber,
Well and true, due to the overwhelming English number.

Bernard was back behind the hill,
Hidden from view of the English, awaiting the thrill,
With him were some fifty-nine other men, gritting their teeth,
Each wearing his surcoat and mail, sword in sheath.

Their horses were restrained,
All urge to commence, here refrained,
Today was the 24th of June, a day worthy, one on which to pray,
So special for the Knights Templar, for it was St.John's Day.

"Three months ago, Jacques de Molay, burned at the stake,"
Said Bernard to those he commanded over, faces awake,
His force of Templar, his knights of valour, their eagerness,
All here today, upon a day they would not miss.

It was not for he, to inspire the three hundred mounted Scots,
For they had prepared themselves, a day of forget-me -nots,
"The revenge we enact today is for him and the Order,
The Order we love so much: our tenet, not the slaughter.

"Not a man shall fight the slightest below his means,
All must fight until victorious, amidst these hilly greens,
And if God should decide to turn a blind eye upon us this day,
We shall not be discouraged, we shall not say nay.

"We will not retreat, but fight until the very last,
We either live to win or die fighting, as in the past,
We give our best, never the worst,
Fight as the devil, as though cursed.

"The Scottish have taken us in when others have not,
Some have dishonoured us with cold stares and horrid plot,
Some have closed the door,
Bridges to, no more.

"This ground has been chosen by Robert the Bruce,
Ground which shall be our saviour, saved from noose,
He chose this ground, and for good reason,
He has been empowered with a vision.

"One where freedom will be won this very day,
One, for the English, filled so grey,
We shall provide unconditional assistance in all he does seek,
Together we are strong and never weak."

The speech slowed, noise falling upon them from the bank,
A sudden drawing-of-attention there, from the flank,
Approaching, one hundred pony boys, followers of the camp,
Armed with pitchforks and clubs, behind the ears a little damp.

Variety amongst them, from all over the country they stem,
Not a single Templar saw reason to laugh or mock them,
The pony boys pushed up level with the Templars stare,
Both as different as apples and oranges, nought to compare.

They were not of the same field,
Carried no shield,
Had never experienced true combat,
Of killing they were thin, soon to be fat.

Their ponies varied in size,
If won at a fair, a poor prize,
They displayed riding skills somewhat... inferior,
Compared to their allies, compared to the Templar.

"These men, here, will be called to battle before us,"
Said Bernard to his band of brothers with little fuss,
"They shall keep busy the English army, their archers,
Allowing us access to king and bodyguard, those… poachers."

A boy rode up and stopped beside Bernard: "They're here,"
Said the boy, "thousands of them," panic rising to ear,
"Yes," said Bernard, "I can hear them; I feel the ground shake,
As they march into position; their final resting place to make."

The boy was stunned: what to do: who knew,
"They're so many, we're so few."
Said Bernard: "Your army is tested and has little fear, "
The boy looked over to the lads on ponies, all so near.

"We're no match for the English."
Calling upon self, a death wish,
"Boy, listen to me, " said Bernard,
"And in your heart you shall see.

"There's as much courage in that formation of ponies,
As there is in that English army of... that despicable species
You'll be riding with the Templar, and Scottish clans, today,
Each and every one has his heart, ready to lay.

"But your duty will see to it that the battle is won,
Now go about and report to duty, Scottish son,
Go stand by your fellow man, ready your ponies for motion,
As your other three hundred Scots on horse ready for action."

The young lad turned aside,
He would perform, he would ride,
And across the table, Bernard looked Guillaume in the eye,
Whom prodded for more, wishing to hear, seeing truth, no lie.

"The battle raged amidst screams of defeat and valour,
The two armies displayed great courage, hour after hour,
And each was on the brink of exhaustion, amidst much gore."
"What happened next?" asked Guillaume, eager to hear more.

"The melee between the Scottish and English was ferocious,
Clutched in fierce fighting, sometimes atrocious,
Unable to break what seemed to be an extended stalemate,
Grinding body across an endless windlass as it does grate..."

Robert the Bruce turned to his squire: "Get ready to kill."
The order was passed on and received by those behind the hill,
To kill the English archers to the very last,
To charge unexpectedly into them real fast.

The ponies and other horse of the Scottish now broke,
Flung themselves into battle, ready to mangle and choke,
Ready to parry and slice,
Ready to hack and dice.

The English were now engaged on each and every side,
Which counted the most for the Scottish as they did ride,
With the greatest satisfaction Robert gave one final order,
Unleashed the Templar of their bonds, of fighters the bolder.

The fury of battle could be seen in all their eyes as they rode,
They could smell victory, see the prize, English to erode,
The sudden impact, the thunderous hooves, much to prove,
A vast number of horses and men, all on the move.

The sound reverberated, struck the ears of the English,
And they stopped seemed to freeze, courage did vanish,
Fear enveloped them all,
They were soon to fall.

They could see the banners flying high above the crest,
From beyond the hill before them, too much to digest,
Through the throng, screams of warning and apprehension,
From nearby comrades, fear spreading, much apprehension.

The Beauseant was unfurled, allowing to move in the breeze,
And it moved, a ballet seemingly performed, victory to tease,
Such a sight, gracious and sublime,
Most high and mighty, and prime.

The Beauseant was half black and half white,
A war standard to dwarf all others, as was its right,
Carried by a single man who was known throughout the ranks,
As the bearer of death: the Balcanifer, to him goes thanks.

The sight of the man and flag above put instant fear into all,
The hearts of all within the English army began to stall,
It was a sight hard to be believed as it neared,
It was as though a ghost had appeared.

It was an apparition, too ghastly to look upon and digest,
Here amidst Edward's army, striking fear into the bravest,
Were the most terrifying of all combatants,
Amongst the English came lofty cries, a variety of sonants.

Other banners could also be seen,
As though dancing alongside the Beauseant as it lean,
As though bodyguards doing their duty, no schism,
Supporting the one and only true semblance of heroism,

Edward could now clearly see before him the battle being lost,
H is men beginning to waver, and the inherent cost,
A growing fear that continued to mount within the ranks,
And to the Templar the Scottish do give their thanks.

The Beauseant, the Beauseant; there it is, flying high,
The symbol of good and bad: no one can deny,
Good and pure to all those of Christian faith and fashion,
The arrival of death to those of Muslim persuasion.

In full regalia the knights continued on into the fray,
The sea of melee before them ceasing, men beginning to pray,
Men stopped to view the passing of this monstrous beast,
Cross of red flying above Grail Knights, on flesh to feast.

Bernard could see up front, men pushed into battle's stench,
Thrusting upon the enemy with vigour, more than if a wench,
Making for the thick of battle, towards the king, his defence,
To slaughter the bodyguard, not here to pay penance.

And the shield of protection gave way,
The strongest of the strong not wishing to stay,
All giving into fear as the common soldier began to flee,
The enemy being brought down upon its knee.

Screams of death erupting from them, filling the air,
Horses of the Knights Templar, their nostrils did flare,
They all pushed, ever on into the thick of war, so unclean,
Thick with blood, but not the worst Bernard had ever seen.

Bernard knew well that the battle would be decided,
By massacring the English army, no leniency provided,
By chasing down each and every solitary man,
This was all part and parcel of his overall plan.

Is it not also true: Scottish heritage is derived from one source,
From vigorous activity, but of course, of course,
And for such activity you need both a seed and an egg,
Waste not the potential fathers, of this every Scot does beg.

The knights seemed to be swallowed up, got carried away,
Disappearing from the face of the earth as they slay and slay,
Oh, a head seen above the enemy, enemy at the withdraw,
The enemy being routed as easily as one, two, three, four.

King Edward turned unto his special knights,
Five hundred men on horseback, with special rights,
Those that he favoured the most, more than any,
Together, the grip of fear strangled them as it did the many.

They fled ahead of the English army as those on foot fled,
Trampled beneath hooves, and Templar with cross of red,
Each and every one of the English fled the field,
Demoralized to the core, left behind their arms and shield.

Never before had Robert the Bruce witnessed such panic,
The fear spreading so far and wide, to head a tonic,
So fast was the Battle of Bannockburn, so gloriously won,
Seemingly in an instant: good, it was, to see the English run.

Scottish foot gained much ground, soon fell upon the caravan,
English spoils, their many supplies, taken by all the clan,
Their baggage, gold, equipment, armour and arms,
This was now but a simple task, as pitching hay on farms.

During the onslaught that day, not a single Templar was lost,
Not a single one beat an eyelid in fear, having served their host,
For they had confronted much worse in the Holy land,
Each having fought battles against a superior army on demand.

Where their number was miniscule in respect to Bannockburn,
The battle was nothing to them, the tide easy to turn,
With God by their side they had defeated those that tried,
At every turn to oppress them, their freedoms denied.

The English fled the scene so fast, so quickly,
Many thousands of common soldiers killed, and so neatly,
Only thirty-eight barons and knights were counted dead,
They bow lay upon the field, this field of dread.

Chapter Twenty-Two

Bernard fell silent and drew some water in, over his lips,
The men at the table looking upon him like a sinking ship,
They were quiet, drawn to every word,
He was a courageous knight, this de Beauvais, this Bernard.

"You have proved yourself in battle, many times, Bernard,"
Said Guillaume, "I see no lying in anything I've heard,
But of others I can't be too sure."
"Others," queried Bernard, innocently pure.

Guillaume: "Those of the Knights Templar who confessed."
"You mean to say, those that were tortured without rest,
Forced into giving false statements, false evidence, and lies,
To announce misgivings of unforgiving acts, whilst in ties."

"Please, Bernard, even if just for a moment, see what we see,"
Said Guillaume: a scoundrel, one he did not wish to be,
"I've seen reports, too," said Bernard, "of these men,
Many withdrew their confessions, scribed in blood from pen."

"Ah, yes," said Guillaume, "within a month of trial's start,
The Knights Templar having confessed in taking part,
April of 1310: fifty-four men, change of mind they did make,
Withdrew their confessions in order to be burned at the stake."

Said Bernard: "Better to be burned at the stake,
Than to quiver and shake,
Within the hands of torturers,
And their overseers."

Guillaume: "In England, after much refusal to comply,
With the wishes of King Philip, on his request to rely,
King Edward did fold to the sway and poor judgement of elder,
Taking side with the pope, arresting all knights of the Order.

"Edward had them placed into custody in January of 1308,
Clearly, preferring for some reason to be early, not late,
Before the trial had begun in France, before carpet was laid,
Yet you slipped through the door: who gave you aid?"

Bernard: "Being charged and tried are of two different concern,
But England paid for its poor judgement, this they did learn."
Guillaume: "You refer to the battle of Bannockburn,
Who aided you in escape: come, I wish to learn?"

Said Bernard, not answering; "I refer to the battle in question."
"And of your escape? Come, tell us, something for ingestion "
"There were many lying underground, strong pillars,
Defending the righteous name of the Templars.

"I don't know any more than that, of them I am not mutual,
I don't know who they were as group or individual,
And could never again find them, even if I tried,
Said Bernard, "so… instrumental, relative and bona fide."

"Very well, you're believed, " said Guillaume, after a pause,
"I wish to speak on that no more, of them or their cause,
And for now, there's no doubt, from what I have seen this day,
That it is your belief, with your entire soul, it is the way.

"So, you believe the trial of the Templar to be highly corrupt,
Extracting untruths from the Templars, were rather… abrupt,
Though many admit guilt in performing a heinous act,
One they would have been forbidden to perform, a sure fact."

"I have no doubt whatsoever,
My brothers were faced with a grave dilemma,
Right across the face of Europe, in particular, France,
They were promised leniency, at every glance.

"All whom looked, advised that the torture that loomed,
Could be thrust aside, none to be groomed,
If only they confessed to each and every ridiculous charge,
Of sodomy, obscenity and heresy, by and large.

"Few knights I knew, if any, would have cared about dying,
But in the mind of some, torture, and the methods of its plying,
Was simply too heavy a conviction, on which to make a stand,
And this is why so many fell, right across the land.

"Torture would have brought about a confession,
All understood this: there would be no compassion,
And so they told a lie in order to save themselves the pain,
To ask God for forgiveness later on, for salvation to gain."

Guillaume: "Trials in England started before those in France,
In October of 1309, much to finance."
Bernard: "The dates are meaningless to me."
A battle of wits, word against word, to be free, to be free.

"Would you agree that the methods of torture,
Were less.... frivolous, than in France; more... mature?"
"I would not, for format is format."
"And so you despise the King of France for that?"

"I do," answered Bernard, so quickly he reacted,
"You know, confessions extracted—."
"Yes Extracted; that's the word exactly,
And to the flesh of man so costly."

Guillaume rephrased: "Confessions received of many a Knight,
Consisted of forms, from the 'kiss of shame', in God's light,
To spitting on the cross and denying Christ through cursed lip,
And talk; the Templar had a head of three faces to worship."

"I think you refer to the one called, Baphomet," said Bernard.
Guillaume: "Ah, so you know of this, you have heard?
And what about Baphomet; what is there to learn, to see?
Come, Bernard, you have been here awhile now... trust me."

Bernard looked at the walls as Guillaume spoke,
Saw reminder once more: devices of torture, pain to invoke,
Guillaume saw the stare: "You will not be tortured,"
A small assurance: to be trusted… honestly, none assured.

Bernard said: "I'm weary to the bone: I tire."
"We'll continue. Go on, assistance I require."
And so he had little choice,
But to consent, to give voice.

"We have been assailed with accusations of idol worship,
But that's far from truth, truth only torn by the torturer's whip,
Baphomet; It's a combination of two Greek words, joined,
Baphe and metis, 'absorption into wisdom' when conjoined."

"I find it hard to believe that you can relinquish this to me,
So many others have refused it, and yet you are so free. "
Bernard: "No one would refuse it, but it has been hidden,
No, no, no... not a secret kept, not forbidden.

"We do not keep this from the citizens; no such suggestion,
But it is kept from the citizens by the hand of the inquisition,
They wished the knights to be found guilty, branded by shame,
And so they conjured up another meaning to the name."

Said Guillaume: "Some might say it held a different meaning,
Sophia; Greek goddess of wisdom, a worthy personification."
"Yes, some might say that, no harm from innocence to invoke,
But I've also heard of the Atbash Cipher. It's a joke."

Guillaume: "But no one's laughing," and loaded a question,
"Some say that Baphomet is a strong indication,
That the Knights Templar believed Jesus was false, was hated,
Yes; a false prophet and that John the Baptist decapitated.

"That's the real reason you worship the head,
Baphomet means, 'baptism of wisdom', it is easily read."
This question and answer was going forever,
Controlled by the exchequer, running a tethered fever.

"No... no, that's not true. I have nothing to hide,"
Insisted Bernard, hurt badly was his pride,
"The trials have killed off the Templar: head from shoulder,
And I have nothing to gain from defending the Order."

"Yes you do, you have conviction and memory,"
Said Guillaume, "and much honour in your armoury,
But I wish, most earnestly, to ask you something more,
Something that might seem... strange, but I must explore. "

"Yes; go on.... this is a waste of time, bears no fruition,
Though the time is yours: and so I tire at your discretion."
Said Guillaume: "Come, Bernard, for I am almost through,
It's something I touched upon earlier, said to you.

"When Jacques de Molay and Geoffrey de Charney were burnt,
Burnt at the stake, something was quickly learnt,
There was reported to have been a last summons, a great sin,
Molay cast a spell to enhance the powers of the devil within.

"He called for Pope Clement and King Philip to join him soon,
To be before the court of God within the year, a spell, no boon,
This, his last day on earth, calling for justice and punishment,
And now: Pope Clement is dead and the king lives to torment."

"Can't be a summons for the devil, a proclamation heard,
If it's to God's court they are to be called," scoffed Bernard.
"You're right, Bernard. The voice of one's song changes,
As it passes from ear to ear, far afield, across ranges.

"What one person hears might not be the same as another."
Bernard: "And so you think that King Philip is in danger,
And furthermore that I should care?
Such a hazardous speech, rather laughable, I say, I so dare. "

Guillaume: "It's different than that; more difficult."
Bernard: "Please, explain this to me, try and hone a result."
"Alright, and here it is: it is clear to us all here,
That the Grand Master of the Order, as he does adhere...

"Of the Knights of the Temple of Solomon, to be certain,"
Said Guillaume, "Jacques de Molay, and his closest subaltern,
The Preceptor of Normandy, Geoffrey de Charney,
Were executed unkindly, and placed upon a sufferable journey.

"King Philip had them removed from their prison cell,
Without the pope's authorisation, on no recourse to dwell,
And ordered them to be taken to an island on the Seine,
Where they were unjustly burnt at the stake as common swine.

"With their deaths went all idea of reforming the Order,
And should I say, none could have been bolder,
And so, wiped out is the Militia of the Temple from Europe,
The head eliminated of its military body, gone all hope.

"Several noblemen spoke out in defence of the Templar,
But these pleas had no effect whatsoever,
Before Jacques de Molay perished in the flames,
He shouted his innocence, spoke certain names.

"He declared that the entire Order was innocent of everything,
Addressing his words to the pope and the king,
The French king is responsible, of this you can have no fear,
For the elimination of the Templar Order, and that is very clear.

"And why? You know this; for their welfare, for good health,
In order to control all of their worldly possessions and wealth,
Little, if any, responsibility should be attributed to the pope,
Now; the king lives, the pope is dead, seemingly gone is hope.

"The Templars were defamed on a massive scale,
Put to death, put to the cross, nail after nail,
It's with these notes of great interest that we now bequeath,
From us to you our interest in this, and for you a new leaf.

'Our forage for information from you, question after question,
Has been an invaluable means to acquire, acquire formation,
All of this in order to understand you more fully,
And so that is it, the answer to that story.

"And so, in the power invested in me,
As exchequer of France, of will so free,
And being of fundamental importance to the people of France,
I request from you your undivided assistance, our only chance.

"For your assistance you shall receive immediate pardon,
From all accusations and untruths, without cordon,
To be set upon the road of your choice,
To be free as you deserve, in one clear voice."

Bernard: "And what is this all about,
What is it that you need from me? Out with it, out!"
Guillaume: "Did you kill the pope?"
Mmmm, at the end of the tunnel? Was there hope?

"I didn't kill the pope: but that does not mean I couldn't,
For the good of the Order… no, it doesn't mean I wouldn't."
They looked around, they believed him wholeheartedly,
Their eyes fell upon Bernard as one, solemn and fixedly.

"There's no doubting you, Bernard; we see much meaning,
And so we come to the reason for this... questioning,
We need something of you, a favour; for country a chance,
We need you to assassinate the King of France."

"Assassinate the King of France?" stammered Bernard,
"You wish me to kill the king?" again, mmm, not so absurd,
And so the questions were a fourage for reason,
That this knight would commit treason.

"Yes," replied Guillaume, pointedly, sharp enough to sting,
"Ricault will go with you. He knows the itinerary of the king,
He knows where he's going to be over the next day or two,
Will you accept this challenge, what we offer, from us to you?"

Bernard thought upon it for a moment, for it all to gel,
Guillaume had orchestrated the reply to be spoken, rather well,
In Bernard's mind the decision had already been secured,
All put before him seemed the fault of one man, senses lured.

He had fought hard battles and lived through hell,
Had story upon story, much to tell,
All, brushed aside by the king, as though… common fodder,
So that the Templars' wealth could be secured, it to squander,

The wealth would do better in the hands of the exchequer,
Although he couldn't be relied upon; no less, but better,
Yes, he was the better option when stacked against the king,
He was the better option between the two: the better for airing.

Bernard looked into the eyes of all around,
Their silence was all to be found,
And then glanced at Guillaume: "I accept."
And it would become a secret, guarded and well kept.

Chapter Twenty-Three

29th November, 1314. Bernard and Ricault stood in the cold,
Upon a well-worn track as the carriage rolled,
The one they had just vacated, no more comfort within,
Now found a slight mist, though did not persist, being thin.

Away into the distance it raced and rolled,
The team of horses spurred on, sturdy and bold,
Trained horse, performing well for their task at hand,
Nostrils now flaming with perspiration, racing across the land.

They both watched as the carriage disappeared from view,
A lantern alight upon the front of the carriage, slightly askew,
Light shifting slightly from left to right,
Leaving the two men behind in poor light.

Now silence came,
Time for the game,
Time for work to begin,
Time to commit their sin.

They opened their ears to the forest around,
The dead of night eerily found,
With a little mist here and there,
Possibly an owl: and likely there to stare.

They stood, silent, solace bestowed upon them both,
Now was the time, for them to commit, possibly to loath,
They each carried a small bundle: some food, water, a blanket,
Nothing heavy that would make a racket.

Bernard carried a longbow and a sword hung from his hip,
Ricault had a crossbow, easy to arm, quick to equip,
Bernard simply hoped that Ricault knew how to employ it,
For such a weapon as that needed more than a quick wit.

Fortunately, here, both men knew the characteristics of each,
Knowledge was one thing, practical application hard to teach,
Knowhow and application, vastly different, beasts to be tamed,
Men cannot soften women by kiss alone, but are easily shamed.

An English Longbow, made from yew, had character and spirit,
A longbowman could release ten to twelve arrows per minute,
Arrows could pierce the armour of a knight at great range,
Required great skill to handle, easy to notch, to make change.

The string was made from hemp as it was the strongest,
Also the least elastic fibre available, the best to invest,
The string was soaked in glue as a protection against moisture,
Could stretch under great pressure, much to endure.

The crossbow, on the other hand, had a wooden stock,
Generally made from yew ash, hazel or elm, a mechanical lock,
Was coated with glue or varnish,
Other than range, no word could tarnish.

A quarrel was laid in a groove on the top of the stock,
The trigger pulled to release the shot, to release the lock,
It had a range of three to four hundred yards, vastly acute,
But could only be shot at a rate of two bolts per minute.

"It makes me homesick," said Bernard, with lack of ado,
"Oh, to hear the birds singing in the trees as they do."
Ricault, whether sarcastic or not: "I hear not a single bird."
"I'm being metaphorical, you coagulated curd."

"You can call this home once more, if you like,
After the king is dead, after the killing strike,
With what we can do for you, and with just as much ease,
You'll be able to go where you like and live as you please."

"The gold you've offered is payment enough: for a pauper,
I feel as a peasant once more; alone, no wife, son or daughter."
"It's payment you'll only receive if you should succeed,"
Reminded Ricault of the exchequer's dying need.

Bernard looked around as they both stood there,
After a minute, time to be formally fair,
He asked: "Are we waiting for some one: or something?
Or do you intend to stand here all day and do nothing? "

"Yes," said Ricault as the beginning of day,
At that very moment, at their feet to lay,
Sprang an unveiling to come; the lighting; the dawn,
Warmth to soon envelope them, to slowly spawn.

From across the treetops it came,
The lighting of the day, all days the same,
And a few birds began to sing,
"Ah, there's your birdsong, song they bring."

Said Bernard: "Ah; waiting for the birds, sound to ripple:
Look, I thought this would have been rather simple,
Go in through a window, slash the king's throat,
And get away whilst whistling a tune, with time to gloat."

"Have you ever been here before, Bernard, to this region?"
"No; of course not. What an absurd question,
Do I look like the king's mother: how rude,
Do I look as though I tend his fields, his forest, his mood?"

"Then you'll have to put your trust in me, trust me true."
"I think I've put more trust in you and... you know who,
Bernard did then say:
"To be granted more than you're willing to pay. "

"I'm glad that you've taken the advice,
Forgotten 'His' name; oh, to be listened to, so nice,
It shows me that you can be trusted,
That you're acquainted with orders, so well adjusted."

"Then your interrogation has paid well."
And the statement was wasted, it fell,
Ricault looked around a little more,
For information to arrive, of something to score.

"I'm waiting for an invitation, you see,
Grasp a better hold on where they may be,
This forest is property of the king,
Not just a home from which the birds can sing.

"As you might well appreciate,
It's very large indeed, and I need to evaluate,
But to change the subject, whilst I'm waiting,
You think you deserve more than we're paying?"

Said Bernard: "It's a simple observation,
Of simple service, not desperation,
Everything I've done was for king and country,
For all of Christendom: all women, all children, and gentry."

"You've served better than anyone, this I know,
Exemplary service, great example you did sow."
Ricault then fell silent,
"Did you hear that? Our agent? "

"No," answered Bernard: "I didn't hear a thing."
"Are you deaf, tuned to hear only the birds as they sing?"
"Maybe my hearing isn't as astute as yours,"
Answered Bernard, sarcastically, one of his flaws.

"You've seen this," and pointed to his right ear,
Scar tissue around the inside, a reminder of battle to wear,
A reminder of his courage in Acre: or somewhere else,
He couldn't recall the place, the battle, the rage, the impulse.

Said Ricault: "You've a good ear remaining, use it,
Come; this way," and he stepped off with spirit,
Bernard followed close behind,
"What did you hear; if you don't mind? "

"It sounded like a horn. It might be our opening,
He hunts early, some days: rather desperate for a king,
Bernard: "In the middle of the night?"
"It's early morning," corrected Ricault, "get it right."

And then: "...or it could have been the wind."
His mind temporarily separated, to prescind,
"If we're going to chase wind all morning, in dark and light,
Then we're going to be here all day and for the night."

"Just as well we each have a blanket," said Ricault,
A whimsical reply, a comical result,
A little breeze then whipped up from nowhere,
And again a sound could be heard, far off but fair.

Bernard looked to Ricault; "I heard it that time. "
"You see," said Ricault, "God is on our side, even in crime."
"What amazes me is you have an insider willing to provide,
The king's location in such a large forest, as though a guide."

"If I didn't know any better, I'd say your confidence is poor, "
"Possibly we're the ones being set up, being hunted like boar."
"That's quite understandable," said Ricault, "but I know this:
The informer provided me with knowledge, as was my wish.

"He advised that the king is after a certain prize today,
And such a prize is more abundant, in one area to stay,
To remain in and around this area of forest,
More than anywhere else, this place is the best."

"What prize does he wish to score?"
"Pig, of course; wild Boar."
Ricault said this, looked down at Bernard 's weapon of choice,
"Where did you learn to use that? " he asked in a clear voice.

Ricault: "I'd heard it's hard to master,
Able to wrought much disaster."
"When in Scotland," answered Bernard, "but I must admit,
That I'm not as good with it as you may expect, not one bit.

"The English are true marksmen with this weapon,
Much strength it commands, a bow of good and bad omen."
Ricault: "Then we'll have to get as close as we can,
Do all we can to kill this most evil man."

"Do you realise, strength is not just for distance to mill,
But for punching through armour and scoring a kill?"
"Well, a closer target is better penetrated,"
Said Ricault as they continued on, much to be debated.

A pig suddenly burst from some shrub,
Within arms reach, close enough to rub,
Scaring the hell out of Ricault, as he jumped to the side,
A little humiliation thee, it hard to hide.

"I'm better with the bow than you are at holding your nerve,"
Said Bernard, "able to give the king what he does deserve,"
Ricault: "I hope so: we may only get one shot at King Philip,
We cannot allow this one and only chance to slip.

"Oh, no; not at all,
With our countries back against the wall,
But something more to reflect on, something to be noted,
If you miss, he might become overpoweringly protected."

"I'm hoping to get close enough to use my sword."
"You're crazy," said Ricault, "good Lord!
Maybe you should just use the crossbow,
It's much more accurate, in this you already know.

"You can switch to the longbow afterwards,
Sing a merry tune on his death, sing with the birds."
"Again with the birds; no, we can do this thing together,
We'll deliver the shots simultaneously: it's smart, very clever."

"Ah," said Ricault, "there's a small problem with that."
Bernard stopped in his tracks, the words oppressively flat,
Ricault continued for several more steps before turning,
Slowly he pivoted, to face Bernard, for knowledge, yearning.

"There's something you're not telling me,"
Said Bernard of the obvious, so obvious to see,
"Maybe we should discuss it first,
For the better, or for the worst."

"It can wait," said Ricault, "we don't know for sure,
The predicament of our situation, nor its cure,
Until we find where the king is, the situation exposed,
Until then, I think this discussion is closed."

"Then you should have said nought,
Before you spoke, you should have thought,
So let's say we've found him,
He's in the open, so happy and prim.

"Just over there, a good range for crossbow practice,
And we see our opportunity, to act, with or without malice,
Because the king himself is preparing to kill a pig,
We are ready with an arrow, to let it loose, into flesh to dig."

"I... I won't be with you, Bernard."
And Ricault dropped what was to be his following word,
For the look in Bernard's eye was surprising, to say the least,
For he appeared to be unmoved, a calm-natured beast.

Said Bernard: "I expected so much, when Guillaume spoke,
That he 'looked forward to seeing you', a clue it did invoke,
'In order to await the announcement of the king's death',
I knew the answer, without drawing a breath.

"I thought then, 'ah; I'm to do the dirty work for myself',
And I was right, put out to dry, alone on the shelf,
I suppose I wasn't meant to hear that notion in motion,
I must've had my 'good' ear pointing in your direction."

"Yes, of course, you must have had: and a lesson here taught,
Anyway, our assassination plot will be found out if I'm caught,
Once we see the king then you're on your own,
Myself; I get away before... Philip vacates his throne."

"I can see now why you insisted on bringing the crossbow,
To allow me a larger choice in weapons, security to sew."
Ricault: "You can do this, Bernard; do this thing for all of us,
For France; for Jacques de Molay, without any fuss.

"Don't let his final condemnation of King Philip go to waste;
Don't allow such to be spurned, let it leave a sour taste."
Bernard: "I'm going to do this thing, not for you, but for me,
That's right; not even for France, but for me, to be free,

"Ah, yes; for all of the suffering I have endured,
For all the time on torturers rack, being heinously injured,
For all the suffering,
Which has been for nothing."

"We won't forget this, Bernard; this victorious blow."
"And the world shall never know."
"Do you want history to recall you as 'that' man, for all time,
The one who assassinated the king, the most heinous crime?"

"I suppose not," said Bernard, "I've lived through worse strife."
"No, Bernard," said Ricault, "you've lived a courageous life,
From the moment you were born of your mother, until death,
A life superior to any on the world's stage, of its hearth."

Asked Bernard: "Is there courage in the things I have done?
Is there courage in honouring wisdom, wisdom won,
In the sacrifices made to pledge allegiance to religion?
I've done nothing more than serve God, to be of his legion."

"You've done more than that, Bernard," said Ricault,
"Achieved a much better result,
You are of much value,
Come now; let's continue. "

Chapter Twenty-Four

An hour passed as they continued on through the wood,
Stepping carefully, a slow pace, as they knew they should,
Listening intently for any sign of the king's hunting party,
This, now, their one and only sworn duty.

They felt as though they were rather close, stopped and stood,
When they heard a voice penetrate the forest, the wood,
"Get it, Richard," came the sound of a man's voice,
"Chase him, catch and kill, let us rejoice. "

The sound of laughter could then be heard,
A second vocal, and then a third,
Several of the party found something amusing,
A lowering of the security, a great easing.

Said Bernard: "Sounds like Richard has fallen over,"
"They're quite close," said Ricault as he moved closer,
Stepping towards a tree, he said: "There they are, "
He pointed, "just over there, not very far. "

Bernard looked and saw: "How many do you see?"
Said Bernard, "I see seven, do you agree?"
"I see five... seven... I see an eighth in the background, "
Bernard: "Nine: I see one running back like a hound."

"Ten," added Ricault, "there are ten."
Bernard: "Is that what you see, or simply within your ken,
Possibly what your spy has told you,
Something to argue, or true?"

"That's only what I see."
"So there could be more... Oh, such glee,
The horn you heard earlier would have been for another group,
Possibly preparing to pounce on a pig, upon such to swoop."

Said Ricault: "Unless this party we see had split into two,
And has only just now come back as one, more to do."
"I concur," said Bernard, "the party would have had to split,
But I am not prone to hunting behaviour, I must admit.

"That may be the case for when hunting pig,
I don't see any dogs, small nor big,
That is strange, is it not,
Or are they simply hard to spot?"

"You will, but not many," said Ricault, rather confidently,
"Our 'friend' saw to it that the dogs were fed, individually,
They were each given something last night,
But he couldn't incapacitate all of them, as he might."

Bernard gave Ricault a rather strange look,
To try and see him for real, to read him as a book,
Ricault: "The driver of our carriage advised me so,
Prior to departing upon his way, he told me what he did know."

Bernard looked up and saw a dog,
As he ran and jumped over a log;
Ricault: "There's one, coming fast, past that man to the rear,
There'll be two or three: that's Richard: have no fear."

"At least you're well informed, if nothing more,"
Said Bernard, considering what may be in store,
Watching as the party of ten took a look at the game,
A pheasant they'd killed, not a pig, hah, hardly the same.

"I'm supposing that they're all armed and are good shots."
"I would think so, but not as good as the English or Scots."
Agreed Ricault, feeling the apprehension in Bernard's voice,
Here to do a job, one may say by little choice.

Bernard looked into Ricault's eyes, spoke rather plain;
"I'm going to wait for the party to split up again,
I think I can then kill them, one by one,
Oh, what joy, what exasperating fun."

"What, we do not seek that result?"
"Keep your voice down, Ricault."
Ricault looked towards the party of ten and back again,
"You wish to kill all of them? isn't that rather vain? "

"I can kill them, one at a time, it's only fair,
So that none of them becomes aware,
I'll then get a close shot at the king, unrestrained,
For us both, much to be gained.

"And if you fail with the first shot then the king shall live,
And we'll never receive another opportunity: none to give."
Bernard considered this,
And the opportunity he did not wish to miss.

"You might be right, but not overly fair,
But you have to agree, our concerns we must share,
The best time to strike will be when the group is split,
I do not know these men: are they quick with wit? "

"Maybe, maybe not,
But somehow I agree to give it a shot,
Bernard: "Again, which one is your friend?
To kill him would be to offend."

Ricault looked out through the forest to the clear ground,
As the party of ten moved on, a pig to be found,
Moving into a thicker part of the land around,
Now rather silent, making little sound.

"I think... yes, do you see the one to the rear?
The one which the dog is now near?
He's glancing around at all of the other,
He's a red scarf and a hat with a feather."

"I do," said Bernard, "I'll make sure he does live,
A promise to you, one that I give."
Bernard looked to Ricault, "will you go now,
To the day will you silently bow?"

"I should," said Ricault, "but... I think I'll stay awhile longer,
My ethics, my thinking, it's all rather stronger."
"Very well," said Bernard and they slowly continued,
"You're the one to face Guillaume, the one to be rescued."

Chapter Twenty-Five

The two men remained downwind from the dogs and group,
The hunters never knew they were there, as they stoop,
They, nor the dogs, could appreciate the lingering danger,
That which loomed so close, at the hand of a stranger.

They were hunting dogs, not dogs bred for combat in a ring,
Not real guard dogs of any description, no savagery to bring,
This weighed heavily in Bernard's favour,
Those pitiful dogs and men of no real valour.

One of the dogs lifted its head, its ears erect,
It looked bemusedly towards Bernard and Ricault, to inspect,
One of the hunting parties men, Conrad, did then mention,
Seeing that something had gained the dog's attention.

"Your majesty," said Peter to the king,
"Over to the left, I think we have something for the taking."
"Good," said the king, "Peter; flush it out,
Take Raymond and Isaac, and if successful, give a shout."

The king looked to another behind,
“Pierre; go with them, something to find.”
Pierre nodded acceptance,
The party was split, now was their chance.

“See Pierre,” said Ricault, of warning, a word,
“Our accomplice? ” asked Bernard,
“If we’re to get help, then it’s from him, he’s our man,
Watch as he follows the others, as close to the rear as he can.”

“Look at him,” said Bernard, “he’ll give us away,
He keeps glancing about; far too suspicious, wouldn’t you say?
He’ll give us both up,
Before I’ve had a chance, this evening, to sup.”

“The king’s too stupid and arrogant,
To know anything different,
He’ll think Pierre is looking for game,
If he can even recall his name.”

“That’s three of them, there,” said Bernard,
“I can kill those three quite easily, just say the word.”
Ricault: “You’re crazy. You’re not on a picnic with your wife,
If you fail, we’ll be in terrible strife.”

“It’s easy for me, forget it, wipe the sweat from your brow,
Besides, you should be going now,”
“It’s not my decision to go,” responded Ricault with no delay,
“I’ve been given instructions by Guillaume, but... I’ll stay.”

Bernard said: "Stay if you want: or quit,
Guillaume won't know anything of it."
Ricault looked into Bernard's eyes: "Just as the country,
It won't know the assassin, for you written will be no poetry."

"It's for you to decide whether the world should know or not,
For I don't care," said Bernard, "so long as I get my shot,
As for the king… with you and Pierre on my side...
How can I fail? You've been a fantastic guide."

"You're right, of course," said Ricault, "I won't be leaving,
I'll stay, and possibly later do a little grieving."
Bernard smiled: "You've just this minute filled me with trust,
We're destined for success, succeed we must."

"Look; they're coming right for us, straight a head,
Our chances of success are diminishing, to be put to bed,
This king will get away," said Ricault, "we're losing our grip,
We must act now and avoid a sinking ship."

Bernard looked around: "Quick, give me that small rock."
Bernard took this and flung it to his flank, to Ricault's shock,
The dog's ears pricked, it looked over at the disturbance,
A noise from within thicket, gaining his attention, a nuance.

Someone from the king's party pointed to this fact,
That the others had changed direction, changed tact,
The king then wandered off to try and encircle possible game,
To encircle what Peter was moving towards; his claim.

Bernard said softly: "We can take them out, one at a time,
Time for our action, time now be ready, time to prime,
We have to be quick, no time to spare,
I can kill the one in front of your man Pierre.

"You take the next in line: be fast, be blunt,
If Pierre is smart then he'll take out that one up front."
"That's Peter," said Ricault, fully aware,
Bernard looked Ricault in the face: "I don't care.

"I care more about Pierre and what he's going to do to help,
What aid will he give in this situation; be brave or yelp."
Pierre was once more looking from left to right,
Not appearing exceedingly bright.

Said Ricault: "Pierre knows something is amiss."
Bernard gave a wave to Pierre, one he could not dismiss,
Ricault forgot himself and pulled at Bernard, warning to serve,
"What are you doing? You 're killing my nerve. "

"No one can see," said Bernard, "and Pierre does now know,
He knows we're here, with our trusty bow,
Get your weapon ready, Ricault, stay calm,
"I'm ready, I'm ready, you have no cause for alarm."

Bernard looked down at the crossbow,
"So you are," and with that he notched an arrow.
"Wait," said Ricault, "Pierre is moving... the man to his front,
I see him getting out his knife, being audaciously blunt "

Ricault: " Look, he's going to kill that man,"
"Quickly, we need to change our plan,
You aim for the one in the middle,
I'll get Peter, and now is not the time to be addle."

With not a further word being said, the two assassins stood,
From behind the cover they had, within the sparse wood,
Pierre could see, knew where to look as the continued the hunt,
Within seconds had closed the gap towards the man in front.

Pierre was saying something to him, to draw his attention,
Pointing off into the distance, a neat little distraction,
Suddenly he plunged his knife into the man's back,
Covered the mouth with his hand, no strength did he lack.

The man in the centre turned slowly around,
Having heard something unfamiliar, horror to be found,
No sooner did his eyes fall upon Pierre and his action,
And he was dead himself, gone in good fashion.

Bernard killed the last man standing, an arrow easily fed,
Stepped off at a fast pace towards the three men now dead,
The confused dog, and Pierre, both his new friend,
But they still had much to do, the status quo to amend.

Pierre looked down at the bodies of Isaac and Raymond,
Beside Bernard, that Templar now a vagabond,
Pierre was looking around: "Ricault; it's good to see you,
I was concerned, I didn't know what to do. "

"This is Bernard," introduced Ricault, "and you did well."
"I'm happy to meet you," said Pierre, more to tell,
"We don't have much time, the party will soon return,
And some of them have smarts, are quick to learn."

"There are three of us now," said Bernard, looking at the sun.
Said Ricault: "And there's only supposed to be one,
But the trees block the rays of the sun, so to speak,
Glare may impede those returning, make their vision weak."

"Now is no time for lessons," said Pierre, "I've done too much,
Of my character this is simply out of touch,
More than I thought I would...
Far more than I actually should…

"I want nothing more to do with this than I have to,
I have a family at home, much to do."
"You're in it now," said Bernard, retrieving Peter's horn,
And put it to his lips, blew hard, of fighting reborn.

The dog sat beside him, no seeker of glory,
"Whose dog is this; mmmm; what's your story?"
"The king's, but he has little to do with its feeding or training,"
Said Pierre: "The others will come; pig their thinking.

"Go to them," instructed Bernard, "say whatever you wish,
And take up a position behind them, death ready to dish,
To dish out your anger one more time, of such do not refrain,
You'll have to kill again."

"I can do this, but I want a reward; I require your agreement."
He looked to Ricault for some form of acknowledgement,
Ricault nodded his head: "I'll see it, but it won't be thrilling,
Guillaume's not going to be happy about all of this killing."

"He'll be satisfied, with his hands on the Templars' fortune,
Go, Pierre, we'll be on the flank, ready for life to prune,
You must strike first, as you did before, your future to fix,"
Pierre nodded his head, ran off towards the other party of six.

The dog followed on,
Not knowing if anything was wrong,
Pierre, to sing a song,
He'd be rich, before long.

Chapter Twenty-Six

King Philip saw Pierre running forward,
"What is it; what's wrong?" he asked of his steward.
"Nothing, your majesty," said Pierre, "they have several pigs,
Caught up in some brush, amidst many twigs and sprigs."

The king looked down at his, quietly admissive dog;
"Why's this animal not with them, still as a log?"
Said Pierre: "I don't know, your majesty, in all to be fair,
Maybe the dog's scared, worried of the pig's lair."

"The king's dogs, scared," said Conrad, a laugh so spent,
"If I didn't find it funny, I'd find it insolent."
"Peter has asked that we approach from the rear,
To prevent the pigs from escaping, made it quite clear."

"I must protest," said Marquis, no advice too hasty,
"That would jeopardise the king's safety;
Your majesty, we must approach from a flank, with care,
Any stray shot from the front could be fatal amidst this glare."

The king looked up and bravely said: “No,
We’ll do as Peter has requested, he’s in the know,
He has good vision,
We shall follow his persuasion.”

“I must insist, your majesty, that you stay to the rear,
Two parties coming together... I hold much fear.”
“It will be fine, Marquis,” said Philip, “I’ll stay to the rear,”
And all of a sudden Pierre felt a cold rush of fear.

Yes indeed, a great amount of apprehension fell upon him,
If he was to kill the man to the rear, kill him so trim,
He would have to kill the king himself: the man, to slaughter,
This assassination was wrought with misfortune and disaster.

Chapter Twenty-Seven

Said Ricault: “It won’t be long now, before the show,
And there they are,” he pointed, “get ready your bow.”
“I might be deaf,” said Bernard, “but I’m not blind.”
As he stepped up from behind.

Ricault: “They each carry a weapon at the ready.”
Bernard: “We hold the initiative, stand steady,
We’ll do the same as before,
Unprepared, they are, for what’s in store.”

“Wait,” said Ricault, “look; see what I see,
King Philip. He’s at the rear, near that moss-covered tree.”
Bernard looked with eyes wide: “I guess your man, Pierre,
Will be the one to kill the king, to give him death’s stare.”

“But will he?” said Ricault, quite unsure,
“That’s the plan,” said Bernard, nervousness to endure,
“The plan was for you to assassinate the king,
Not for Pierre or myself to be involved with this thing.

"Pierre knows these men well,
Hard it will be for a scenario to sell,
They would have reported the incident as an accident,
Not as an assassination. But now there will be no argument."

"It can still be reported as such," said Bernard,
"If Pierre delivers: we kill them all, every man and steward,
Pierre can still make a report,
But whatever happens, we do not abort.

"No one will believe that a single man killed a party of nine,
To survive without a scratch, to be perfectly fine,
Besides, the king's death will record a lie,
The people will be denied the truth: deny, deny, deny."

"Your right," said Ricault as he continued to observe,
"I just hope that Pierre has the insight and the nerve."
"He'll have two things going through his mind at the present;
Guilt, and extra reward for doing good service, it to be spent."

Chapter Twenty-Eight

Pierre was nervous to say the least,
Ready to release, from within, the beast,
The party drawing closer to the area of concern,
No pigs to be seen, much misery to learn.

Pierre closed the gap towards the king,
Placing his hand upon the hilt of his knife, death to bring,
The king suddenly turned upon Pierre: "Where are they?"
Pierre removed his hand from the hilt: "There they lay."

He pointed for the king to see,
But clarification was not to be,
One of the dogs pricked up its ears, a growl clearly heard,
Giving a sense of direction towards Ricault and Bernard.

Said Bernard "The time is now or never,
Are you ready, Ricault, with an arrow from quiver?"
Ricault: "I'm ready, and when I hear the twang of your bow,
I'll shoot upon them a shattering blow."

“Steady now,” said Bernard, “have no fear,”
As Pierre made his move towards the king’s rear,
“He’s almost there,
Be ready to shoot firm and fair.”

“Look!” yelled Richard, “I see something.”
And a great calamity this did bring,
“The body of one of the others,” said Ricault,
“Wait for Pierre,” insisted Bernard, “wait for a result.”

Pierre was a step away from the king,
Removed his knife from its sheath, the blade to sting;
“What is it?” demanded the king as he stopped in his tracks,
The air still silent, from arrows no whacks.

Richard turned and saw Pierre almost fall over the king;
“Your majesty! Behind you!” alert to ring,
Pierre wasn’t expecting the king to stop dead on the spot,
The knife penetrated King Philip, but deadly, it was not.

A look of horror fell upon the king, a look void of grace,
As he turned with the startled look of pain upon his face,
The knife was withdrawn. Pierre then pushed with all his force,
The knife slid effortlessly into the king’s gut, death to endorse.

“Murderer!” yelled Richard, alerting the rest,
His voice echoing throughout the forest,
The others turned, saw Richard lift his weapon and let loose,
To kill Pierre, as Bernard and Ricault revealed the ruse.

Pierre stood shocked, open mouthed, staggered back and fell,
The quarrel from Richard's weapon had pierced him well,
Just to the side of his throat,
Blood seeping to cover his coat.

But such a wound could be easily mended,
If gotten to quickly, and hence attended,
And eager not to draw further attention,
Pierre remained upon the ground, encased in apprehension.

Ricault thought now of himself: Pierre was no 'great' friend,
Nothing now but consideration for his own life to defend,
As for Bernard, he had no time to make any such wild guess,
Of the situation, upon his mind, he did quickly assess.

The king fell to his knees: "Help!" grasping his wound firm,
The knife fell from his blood-soaked hands as he did squirm,
Wriggling there upon the forest floor,
In much pain, too much to ignore.

The two men in front of the king fell dead,
Accurate shooting from Bernard delivering much dread,
They were both to be forever, no more,
And the king gasped for air as he sought assistance, as before.

"Marquis; Richard!" yelled Ferrario, getting low, upon a knee,
He brought his bow into line with his eye, target to see,
Pulling back with all his strength, the short bow that he carried,
An arrow placed, ready to fire, but with death to be married.

"Protect the king!"
A call to arms to sing,
Bernard released another arrow,
It pierced the head of Ferrario.

Ricault and Bernard were now safely behind a tree,
As an arrow flew, wild and free,
It hit and embeded within the trunk so large,
Marquis hence missing, no other available to charge.

Ricault pulled the string of the crossbow back,
Slid into place another bolt, to continue with the attack,
By the time he was ready to fire his second shot,
Bernard had a fifth ready to release, one more to allot.

The assassins looked out to their front, target to be found,
King Philip was lying somewhere upon the ground,
He couldn't be seen, but could be heard as he screamed,
Richard and Marquis also hid from view, or so it seemed.

"Where are they?" asked Ricault, to hence be chasten.
"Quiet, fool," scolded Bernard, "listen."
It wasn't long before gasps of injury and assault came to ear,
From the king as he cried for assistance, for aid to appear.

"Whoever is alive, I need assistance this minute,"
Cried Philip, "I need assistance, damn it."
Marquis was about to make a move and Richard stopped him,
"No, Marquis; wait, or your fate will be grim."

Bernard released his arrow and towards Richard with ease,
Through some tall grass which shifted in the slight breeze,
Richard's head momentarily popped up above the grass,
Before it fell from view, another life to pass.

Bernard lowered his weapon, burden now light,
"If my calculations are right,
We have but one target that does remain,
Just a single one, one little stain."

"Two," said Ricault, "we also have the king."
"I saw Pierre stab him," said Bernard, clarity to bring,
"He won't be in any condition to fire an arrow, to fight back,
Of true conviction and ability he will truly lack."

"Yes," agreed Ricault, "you're right, as you say."
Ricault looked out towards where the dead lay,
"Marquis... is your name Marquis?"
The tone of his voice: compassion; the ticket, the key.

Marquis was silent, concerned for longevity, for health,
But calmed, and through sheer fear, revealed himself,
From the slight hollow in which he was currently hiding,
"Yes; that's my name," ah; deciding on ceding.

"Am I correct in assuming that you are the assistant,
Assistant to King Philip, directly, and in duty, persistent?"
Philip could hear the exchange of words as he lay there in pain,
Listen he must, for there may be substance of chance to gain.

"Yes," answered Marquis, "that's correct. Who are you?"
"Let's just say that assassins 'do as they do',
Their role in life is to know of their intended target,
And not the target to know the assassin, none to beget."

Bernard continued: "and that furthermore,
You are not that target, Marquis, of this you can be sure,
All we want is the king,
You have a chance of life, instead of dying."

"I... I can't do that," said Marquis, "of his life I cannot sell."
Bernard: "If you give the king up then I will reward you well."
Added Ricault: "The king is all we wish for,
His life for yours, and nothing more."

"Don't listen to him, your fool," said Philip,
"Your life is not theirs, but is in my grip,
I'll have you strung up and tortured,
Quartered and flayed, heinously butchered."

"Do you hear that?" said Bernard, "we are two, you are one,
Your days on earth are numbered, of choice almost none,
The king will not sit favourably with you by his side,
With him and his rule you should not abide.

"You're nothing to him, of this you can see,
Reveal yourself and you will be set free,
Put down your weapon,
You should no longer be here, you we do not threaten."

"No, please," pleaded Philip, "don't make the wrong choice."
Said Marquis: "I hear honesty within your voice,"
And he slowly stood up from where he hid,
On his whereabouts he did lift the lid.

Bernard released his last shot which struck Marquis,
Right through the heart, target so easy to see;
"What! Damn you!" yelled Ricault,
Such treachery was an insult.

"You hired me for a job and that job is almost done,"
Said Bernard, "and hence, we have almost won,
Come; let's talk with the king,
Let's go listen to him sing."

Chapter Twenty-Nine

The two men looked down upon the form of King Philip,
Lying there upon the forest floor, as life did slip,
Blood was everywhere, gut wound severe,
And Ricault looked briefly around, did not even leer.

Ricault was looking for any sign of Pierre,
Surely he was dead; of misfortune he'd had his share,
And then, suddenly, from deep down, seeking final result;
"Kill him now and be done with it," ordered Ricault.

"No, please," said Philip, "I'll make it worth your while,
If you keep me alive, that is," and attempted a smile.
Bernard: "Look at those eyes, Ricault. You're an imposter,
How was it, when you killed the Templar Grand Master?"

"I didn't kill him," pleaded Philip, again he lied,
"I... I wanted to save his life but it was too late... I tried."
"Why do you have to lie like that?" said Bernard.
"Come on; hurry up," insisted Ricault, his final word.

"You make me sick," said Bernard, "you filthy swine."
"I'm the king," said Philip, of his life, he did define.
"You're not my king," and in a flash, not wishing to gloat,
He withdrew his sword and plunged it into Philip's throat.

The gurgling sounds of drowning were heard,
He died in his own fluid, not fever as did the third,
King Philip was dead: "That's it, the job is done,
And hence, your wishes have been secured: you've won."

"Job done, indeed," agreed Ricault, "and now it's time,
Time to get the hell out, away from the scene of the crime,
I could not see Pierre, he cannot be found,
He must surely be somewhere near, upon this ground."

They started walking briskly away from the site of mayhem,
Pierre was moving in the opposite direction, away from them,
He was clasping hard to the wound at his throat,
To report the death of the king, of misgivings to quote.

"Look; there goes Pierre,"
Said Bernard, "look, over there."
Ricault: "Do you think the death will report as assassination?
Or do you think that's out of the question?"

"No; of course not," said Bernard, "that would be awkward,
"It's so much easier to live with the idea put forward,
That he was killed in a hunting accident most grisly,
And that the culprit was punished accordingly.

"The last thing the authority needs is for the truth to get out,
With lack of a guilty party to point at and shout,
I just hope Pierre comes up with a story to save his own neck,
Any proofs would be hard to prove, hard to check."

They now walked towards the place of their disembarkation,
A great number of birds flying overhead amidst a migration;
Bernard could only contemplate where his life was to lead,
For, of his life's restraints, he had finally been freed.

www.ingramcontent.com/pod-product-compliance
Lightning Source LLC
Chambersburg PA
CBHW020142120726
47903CB00007B/2383